dad

A TABOO TREAT

USA TODAY BESTSELLING AUTHOR

K WEBSTER

Dr. Dan
Copyright © 2019 K Webster

Cover Design: All by Design
Photo: Adobe Stock
Editor: Emily A. Lawrence
Formatting: Champagne Book Design

This is a work of fiction. Names, characters, places, and incidents either are the product of the author's imagination or are used fictitiously, and any resemblance to actual persons, living or dead, business establishments, events, or locales is entirely coincidental.

Lauren will do anything besides face reality.

Her truth won't set her free because it's too busy hunting her.

It chases her into the ER more often than she can count.

Dr. Venable is hell-bent on finding answers for his most frequent hospital visitor.

Even when his stunningly beautiful patient is difficult and resistant.

He'll uncover her pain because he wants nothing more than to heal the sassy young woman.

Long nights.

Rising temperatures.

Feverish needs.

They spend more time than ethical on their quest for answers.

His position. Her age. Nothing will keep them apart.

Not until they get what they came for.

Love may not be a cure,
but they're going to test it anyway.

K WEBSTER'S Taboo World

Welcome to my taboo world! These stories began as an effort to satisfy the taboo cravings in my reader group. The two stories in the duet, *Bad Bad Bad*, were written off the cuff and on the fly for my group. Since everyone seemed to love the stories so much, I expanded the characters and the world. I've been adding new stories ever since. Each book stands alone from the others and doesn't need to be read in any particular order. I hope you enjoy the naughty characters in this town! These are quick reads sure to satisfy your craving for instalove, smokin' hot sex, and happily ever afters!

Bad Bad Bad

Coach Long

Ex-Rated Attraction

Mr. Blakely

Malfeasance

Easton

Crybaby

Lawn Boys

Renner's Rules

The Glue

Dane

Enzo

Red Hot Winter

Dr. Dan

Several more titles to be released soon!

Thanks for reading!

K

Matt—love you, honey.

and

Lauren—you're a fighter and an inspiration.
I'm proud to have created a character in your honor.

Note to the Reader

Dr. Dan is a complete standalone. However, if you want to learn more about the other characters in this book, you should start with *Enzo* and then read *Red Hot Winter*. Those two books will give you deeper insight into Daniel's and Lauren's characters.

Hope you enjoy their story!

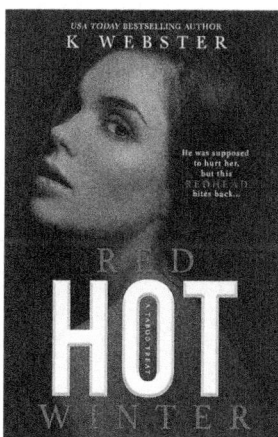

DR.
dan

A TABOO TREAT

CHAPTER
one

Daniel

St. Patrick's Day

"I'll wash your car," Morris says, waggling his brows at me.

Right.

Evan Morris—Brown County Hospital's playboy—doesn't wash cars. He pays people to do that shit for him. If I gave in, he'd pay one of his groupies to do it. Negotiating with Morris takes a helluva lot more calculation on my end. A car wash is too damn easy and he knows it.

The bastard smirks, his blue eyes flashing with mischief. He's fifteen years my junior and I always wonder if I was a smug little shit back then too. I don't remember being a spoiled brat at thirty and I certainly didn't sleep with half the staff at BCH.

Crossing my arms over my chest, I eye him with scrutiny. Silver spoons can't buy muscle mass much to Morris's annoyance. I may be just shy of my forty-fifth birthday, but I annihilate when we go to the gym together. His blue eyes flicker to my biceps that are bulging against the fabric of my baby blue scrubs, causing him to stand a little straighter and to fluff his pretty-boy blond hair that women seem to fumble all over themselves to touch.

"My car is fine," I start, one corner of my lips lifting. "But yours…"

"You can't borrow the 911."

I shrug my shoulders as though I don't care. "Fine, you get the next broken nosed belligerent asshole from Blarney's Bar who'll puke up green beer all over your pretty shoes."

Morris hates puke.

For an ER doctor, that's a problem.

"I hate you, man," he grumbles.

"Aww, why do you hate Dr. Venable?" Chrissy, an ER nurse and one of Morris's newest bedroom conquests, asks him.

He flashes her an easy smile, but I can tell it's not genuine. From what he told me at the gym last week, he fucked and ran because she was clingy as hell. Serves him right. When you sleep with your co-workers, that shit will bite you in the ass eventually.

"We were betting on who gets to deal with the next drunk patient. If he lets me take his car home tonight, then I'll take them." I shrug and Morris glowers.

Chrissy grips his elbow. "They just brought in a new patient. I'd give him the car for the night," she warns. "Wasted partygoer. Possible alcohol poisoning."

Which means green puke.

"Fine," Morris grumbles. "Greenie is all yours."

"And so is your new 911 Carrera S model. I'm taking her for a spin tonight," I tell him with a victorious grin as I walk backward down the corridor. "I'll pick her up in three hours for our date. Don't wait up for her."

He scratches at his jaw with his middle finger, discreetly flipping me off. I laugh before turning and striding along the squeaky linoleum floors on a mission to meet my next patient in triage. St. Patrick's Day is one of our busier days in the ER. Not as busy as Independence Day or New Year's Eve, but it's up there. Anytime you have a holiday that loosely revolves around drinking, it means you have more careless people getting themselves into all sorts of shit.

But I love my job. Can't complain. I never settled for anything less than the constant excitement of what the emergency room brought in. It varied from sickness to mangled and barely breathing car accident victims. Each time the double doors open and the EMT rushes in, it's a surprise. You don't know which skill you'll utilize that day. I'm not sure I'll ever move into surgery or oncology or become a general practitioner. Doing essentially the same thing day in and day out is boring. Besides, if I had settled into a specific field, I would've probably never met my daughter.

Less than a month ago, a girl walked in looking just like a woman from my past. It was eerie as fuck. Eerie enough that I boldly asked for a paternity test. Turns out, I am the father of an eighteen-year-old girl. And now she lives with me. As strange as it was staring at someone with my same jade-green eyes, it also filled a hole of longing. I've been married to my career for so long, but I've never settled to build a family. For nearly a month now, though, I've been given a daughter and it's incredible. Scary as fuck that I'll somehow mess up this parenting gig, but also cool as hell.

"Dr. Venable," Lin greets, a chart in hand as she bounces up to me.

Lin is barely five feet tall and is built like a child. She may be a nurse, but she's smarter than Morris. And she's never climbed into bed with him, which makes her smarter than the rest of the staff. I like working with Lin because she knows her shit and doesn't goof around.

"Possible alcohol poisoning?" I ask as I scrub my hands at a sink. "That's what Chrissy said."

She rolls her eyes, her chin-length black bob bouncing at the exaggerated movement. "No. The patient says she had one glass, so it's not alcohol poisoning. Chrissy doesn't know what she's talking about."

I frown as I dry my hands. "Rohypnol?" Wouldn't be the first time I had a roofied patient.

"No," she says quickly. "She's aware and can move. More dizzied and dazed than anything. Her blood pressure is 177 over 116."

"Age?" I bark out, already sliding into urgent doctor mode.

"Eighteen."

A flash of panic startles me. Now that I have my daughter, every time a patient comes in with the same age, I worry I'll walk in and find her. The thought of losing her when I just got her is scary as hell.

"That's too high. Name," I grunt out.

"Lauren Englewood."

The relief is brief that it isn't my daughter, Jenna, but the desire to help my patient soon becomes my sole focus. I snag a couple of latex gloves and slide them on before pushing the curtain away to assess my patient.

Her eyes are closed when I enter the room. Pale flesh. Damp blond hair. The young woman is listless and breathing heavily.

"Lauren," I say as I reach her side. "I'm Dr. Venable. How you doing there?"

She flutters her eyes open, revealing intense brown eyes. My gaze skims over her face as I assess her. A few freckles dot her flesh under her eyes and over her nose. Her cheekbones are high, giving her the look of so many of those magazine models who litter the hospital waiting room. I drop my focus to her lips, looking for discoloration. They're not blue or purple indicating something respiratory. Just full and naturally red.

"Lauren?" I ask.

"I'm fine," she breathes out.

I arch a brow at her. "If you were fine, you wouldn't be here. My nurse tells me you only had one drink."

"Yeah."

"Could it have been tampered with?"

She swallows hard. "No, I made it myself."

"Did you feel this way before or after you consumed the drink?"

"Before," she murmurs. "I had a headache, but my brother, Landon, was having a party. I didn't want to ruin it."

Using my stethoscope, I begin listening to her heart. It's steady, but I still want an EKG to be sure. High blood pressure on a patient this young is worrisome.

"You have a headache now?" I ask as I pull the instrument away.

"Pounding, yes," she admits. "And my side hurts."

I loop the stethoscope around my neck. "I'm going to press on your abdomen. Let me know if you feel any pain or pressure."

She nods and I push against her over her shirt. Her brows furrow, but she doesn't wince.

"Is it uncomfortable?"

"I just feel really full."

"I'd like to get a urine sample to run a full analysis—"

"No," she cries out, her hand gripping my wrist. "I mean, I'm fine."

"Again, Lauren, you're not fine. You wouldn't be in triage if you were."

She lets out a frustrated huff and sits up. "See, fine. My dad is out of town and my brother is wasted. I just want to go back home. Give me some Tylenol or whatever. I'm sure it's just a migraine."

"A urinalysis could rule out some things like urinary tract infection or kidney infection. I'd like to run those tests to check for blood in the urine. With your high blood pressure and what you're describing with your abdomen, I want to rule it out."

Her nostrils flare and her cheeks burn red. "I don't have blood in my urine."

I let out a heavy sigh. "I'm just trying to help you. Your blood pressure is through the roof. I want to get to the bottom of this."

Lin peeks her head in, waving a urine cup. "Ready, hon?"

Lauren shakes her head. "I'm not peeing in a cup."

Gritting my teeth, I look over my shoulder at Lin. "Sodium nitroprusside. We'll do a drip to get her blood pressure down along with some fluids. Draw a blood sample and—"

"I'm fine. Just give me the medicine to make this headache go away and send me home. I don't know why Winter brought me here in the first place," Lauren bites out.

"I'll be right back," I tell Lauren before standing and stalking out of the room.

Lin frowns at me. "Hiding something?"

"Yeah. Due to her age and the fact she was partying, I'd like to say it was the fact she also took drugs, but we won't know for sure unless she allows us to run the tests."

"Can you convince her?"

"I'll try. But you know how some people are. We'll get her in a more stable condition and then we can try and convince her from there."

Lin runs off to get the meds and I walk back into the room. I cross my arms over my chest and frown at Lauren. She squirms under my intense glare.

"It's my job to want to treat what's going on with you," I tell her. "The human body isn't something that can be ignored when it's flashing warning signals."

Her brows furrow and she tears her brown eyes from mine. "It's probably a fluke. I'll go see my doctor if it happens again."

I sense a lie in her words, but it's not like I can force her. I'm about to continue my insistence she gets tested when chaos erupts nearby.

"Dr. Venable, you're needed in triage one!" Chrissy calls from beyond the curtain, the frantic edge in her tone indicating I'm about to encounter something bloody.

Reluctantly, I leave the girl.

She may not be in a life-threatening situation just yet, but my gut tells me it's only a matter of time.

CHAPTER
two

Lauren

April Fool's Day

Sweat beads across my brow as I desperately try to ignore the pain lancing through me. Of all the classes to fall ill, my senior English class with Mr. Hanks is the worst one. Neil Hanks is one of my dad's closest friends. He's a tattletale too.

As though he has access to my thoughts, he pins me with his dark brown eyes. His mouth moves as he discusses archetypes in stories, but his gaze is penetrating. If I know Neil, I know he'll send a text to Dad before I even leave the classroom. Then, Dad will fly home from Chicago and baby me. More than baby me…he'll pressure me to see a doctor.

I swallow hard and try not to come off as though I'm suffering in this hard chair. I hate doctors—even good-looking ER ones. They're nosy and they reveal things about you that don't deserve to be learned about. It wasn't long after Mom was diagnosed by doctors that she deteriorated and died. One moment she was here and happy, the next she looked pretty in her favorite church dress lying in an expensive pearl-gray coffin.

Absently, I touch my silver heart necklace. It was Mom's. A Mother's Day gift to her the year before she died. Now it's mine.

The ache inside me no longer belongs to physical pain, but one that comes from the soul. I miss her every day. Dad has thrown his attention into his career and Landon obsesses over his girlfriend, Callie. That's how they cope. I'm still trying to figure out how to cope with her loss.

A wave of dizziness washes over me and I grip the edge of my desk to hold myself steady. Throbbing inside my skull begins pounding in tandem with my heartbeat. I'm soaked with sweat and lightheaded. Closing my eyes, I try to relax but my whole body jerks when I start to slump in my seat. I tense back up and suck in deep breaths.

"Miss Englewood?"

Neil's voice echoes inside my head, forcing me to open my eyes. He blurs and becomes two. A wave of black slicks over my vision, blinding me and dragging me under.

"Lauren!"

I wake to find Neil's worried face searching mine. Several of my peers are huddled around. I'm on the floor of the classroom. God, my head hurts. I reach up to touch my head and Neil shakes his.

"Don't. I think you're going to need stitches. You hit it pretty hard."

Hit?

He pulls away a cloth that's covered in blood before folding it and then pressing it to my forehead again. I'm embarrassed to be lying in my teacher's lap with kids staring at me with worried looks.

"Uh, I'm fine," I whisper.

"Where is she?" my brother barks out, rushing into the room. "Holy shit, Lauren!"

It must be serious because Neil doesn't even get onto him about his language.

"Did you call your dad?" Neil, the tattletale, asks.

"He's looking for a flight right now but won't be in until later. Ambulance on the way?"

Neil nods.

Ambulance?

"I'm fine," I try again, hot tears flooding my eyes. I just want to go home and climb into bed. "It's just period pains."

A few guys make gagging sounds and Landon frowns as he squats beside me.

"Nice try, sis."

I try to scowl at my brother, but it hurts my head. It's annoying sometimes that I have to share my senior year with him. Had he not failed the eighth grade, I could deal with this on my own.

"I got her a Sprite," a girl named Penny says, kneeling beside Landon. But despite my brother being a football hero at our school, her eyes are all for Neil. Gross. Luckily, he ignores her.

They help me sip on the cold drink, but all it does is make my stomach churn. The last thing I want to do is get sick all over my teacher in English class with all the students watching.

"How long was I out?" I ask, blinking away another wave of dizziness.

"Fifteen minutes," Neil says.

A cold sweat washes over me. Fifteen minutes?! Everyone just stared at me for fifteen minutes while I was passed out. Oh my God. I want to crawl into a hole and die.

"EMT is here," someone calls out.

Commotion can be heard as two men roll into the room with a stretcher. My skin burns with embarrassment as the whole freaking class and two EMTs work together to get me situated on the stretcher. As the men assess me while simultaneously strapping me in, I can't help but cringe. This is all a big deal over a bumped head. When Principal Renner shows up, a worried frown on his face, I decide I'd rather just die in this moment. Rather than facing all the curious stares, I close my eyes. By the time I get inside the ambulance, I don't feel any less stressed. With Landon fretting at my side and Dad rushing to get home, I can't help but worry this is all about to get worse.

Landon's fingers fly over his phone as he texts and I focus on the softly murmured words of the EMT as he checks my vitals. By the time we arrive at the hospital and they pull me out, I feel good enough I could just leave.

But no one is letting me leave. The EMT wears a concerned frown as he pushes the stretcher into the ER. He says some things to a couple of nurses and instructs Landon where he can wait for me.

I'm pushed into the same room I visited when I got sick a couple of weeks ago. Great. History is repeating itself. Hopefully I don't have to deal with the same doctor. Heat floods through me. He was so hot and it was so freaking embarrassing.

The nurses take over once they get me transferred to a bed and a familiar Asian nurse worries over my head. She cleans it but doesn't stitch it up.

"Dr. Venable will want to take a look at this. Sit tight. He'll be right in."

I groan as I wait for the good-looking doctor who made me feel like crap last time. He'll pressure me into more tests—tests I don't want to have done.

The curtain is wrenched open, revealing Mr. Sex in Scrubs. My thighs clench because he's too hot to be a doctor. It's unfair. Upon seeing me, his neutral expression darkens. His brows furl over his intense green eyes and his full lips press into a firm line.

"You're back," he says. His deep, gravelly voice flitters over my nerve endings, making me squirm.

"Thought you'd be bored and would need something to do," I sass, irritated that he seems irritated.

His jaw clenches as he approaches. Like before, his gaze scrutinizes my features. When his finger reaches up to push away a strand of hair from my eyes, I tense. He mistakes it for pain because he frowns.

"Your head hurts where you hit it?" he asks as his gloved hands ghost over the cut flesh.

"It's okay."

"Either you have a high pain tolerance or you're skilled at evading," he grumbles.

My eyebrows lift in surprise at his gruff tone. "Do I need stitches?"

"You do. But don't worry, I've been doing this for a long time. It won't leave a scar."

His confidence has me relaxing. This seems to soften his edge because he flashes me a small smile. "Don't go running off yet, Cinderella." He starts to leave.

"I'm sure you'd just chase me and wrangle me back into this bed," I say with a pout.

He jerks his head my way and scowls. It isn't until he leaves that I realize my words could be misconstrued. Images of the sexy doctor pinning me down in bed and taking my virginity are too hot and inappropriate for the ER.

When he returns, his features are impassive. He's quiet as he sets up his supplies to stitch me up. Any time Landon went to the emergency room over football injuries, the nurses always stitched him up.

Getting special treatment from the hot doctor sends a thrill shooting through me.

"Fainting is one way to skip out of class," he murmurs as he begins stitching my wound closed. I sense he's trying to distract me, so I take the bait.

"Mr. Hanks is my dad's friend. No one wants to hang out with their dad's best friend and talk about archetypes in literature."

Dr. Venable smiles at me, revealing bright white teeth. He's handsome enough to be in one of those dental commercials. I wonder if I licked his teeth if they'd taste minty. Biting on my bottom lip, I try to hush the dirty thoughts I have running through my head.

"I guess hanging out in triage arguing with me is much more entertaining," he says with a chuckle. The sound of it—deep and throaty—vibrates down to my core.

"Are you flirting with me, Doc?"

He stiffens and the scowl from earlier is back. "Tell me how you fainted," he orders, all playfulness gone from his features. "What led up to it? How did you feel?"

"I probably just fell asleep because it was so boring," I grumble. "Or maybe it's an April Fool's joke for my teacher."

This man doesn't buy my lies for a second. He continues his task, his hot glare burning me into the bed. His Adam's apple bobs as he swallows. I wonder what the yummy doctor tastes like. His dark brown hair is tousled like he rolled out of bed that way. The gel in it screams that he was going for the effortless look in the first place. I want to reach my fingers up and ruffle through it, messing it up. The scruff on his cheeks is trimmed low and I wonder what it'd feel like to kiss someone with facial hair. Every guy I've kissed has been baby-faced and smelled like Red Bull.

Dr. Venable smells like expensive, manly cologne. Like he doesn't belong in the same realm as those guys I go to school with. I bet he doesn't kiss with a one-track mind to feel my tits up either. He looks like the kind of guy who'd take his time worshiping every inch of flesh.

"I'll take the stitches out in a couple of weeks," he tells me as he cleans up his mess. "Don't mess with it until then."

"Great, thanks. Can I go now?"

His green eyes flicker. "Nope. I'm ordering a CT scan since you hit your head. Don't fight me on this one, Lauren."

Crossing my arms over my chest, I frown, but the pulling on my stitches stops me. "Fine."

He winks at me before exiting the room. That one simple wink turned me into a sweltering ball of flames.

For the next hour, I let Dr. Venable send me to radiology to get the head scan. The woman running the machine is nice and talkative. It makes my head hurt worse. I'm dying to get the hell out of here.

As soon as I'm back in bed, Dr. Venable storms back in, wearing a frown.

"What is it?" I demand.

He lets out a heavy sigh. "Scan looks great."

I scoff at him. "So disappointed, aren't you, Doc?"

"Daniel."

His name on his lips sounds erotic and enticing. Only I would crush over a doctor old enough to be my dad and who is infuriatingly persistent in an area I'd rather forget. My health.

"Okay, *Dr. Dan*," I bite out. "Why do you seem so unhappy about my head being fine?"

He winces at my words. "I'm not unhappy, I'm annoyed."

The nerve. He's supposed to be a doctor!

"What?" I hiss out, trying desperately to hide my hurt.

His features soften as he sits beside me. "I'm annoyed because now I have to argue with you."

"You could let me win."

He tilts his head up toward the ceiling as though he's praying. "Your health isn't a game." He brings his chin down, his green eyes boring into me. "I want to run some tests. You're already here." His head nods at the machines. "Blood pressure is high again. How's your abdomen?"

Oh, hell no. Not falling for this.

"Great," I lie.

His sharp jawline muscles flex as he clenches his teeth. "I could hold you here until your father arrives."

Rather than wincing because I know it'll be easy to convince Dad, I lift my chin and meet Daniel's glare with one of my own. "I was having period pains. Got lightheaded and passed out. I should have eaten more for lunch. My head hurts, but you stitched me right up. I'm ready to go home now."

Our eyes lock in a silent, heated battle.

In the end, I win because he gives me a clipped nod and storms from the room.

So why does it feel like a loss?

CHAPTER
three

Daniel

I'm a stalker. A fucking creep. But I ignore those thoughts as I scroll through Instagram on my quest for answers. It's been nearly a month since I discharged Lauren Englewood into her brother's care after she'd hit her head hard enough to need fourteen stitches. And less than a month since she came in unannounced to have them removed. My mind drifts to the day I took the stitches out.

"You look like you're feeling well today," I mutter as I tower over her, plucking at the stitches with my scissors.

She looks better than well.

I'd gaped like some kind of pervert when she came waltzing into the ER like she owned it moments before. Unlike the other two times I'd seen her, she was dressed and made up. Big brown eyes are more striking with her eyeliner and mascara. Her pouty lips are redder than I've seen them thanks to lipstick. It's her attitude that's different. More fiery than normal.

"I'm feeling great," she tells me. "I have a date."

She crosses her legs and my eyes drop to the way her black dress slides higher up her creamy thighs. My cock reacts and I want to slap the shit out of myself. I'm not Morris. I don't get aroused at work.

"A date, huh?" I grumble as I pull at a loose thread. "Who's the lucky bastard?"

Her lips curl into a wide grin that lights up her whole face. "You almost sound jealous, Dr. Dan."

I glower at her. "You're a kid. Hardly."

"I'm not a kid," she bites back. "And his name is Rex."

"Rex sounds like a prick. Be careful."

She laughs, the sound sweet and sexy all at once. "You are jealous!"

"I have a daughter your age," I grumble. "Call it fatherly instinct to protect."

"I won't call you Daddy, Doc. I already have one of those."

I jerk my hand back to glare at her. "Stop."

"Stop what?" Her big brown eyes widen, feigning innocence. When she bites on her bottom lip, I have such an intense urge to kiss her, I have to physically take a step back so I don't act on my desires.

"Besides your head, how are you feeling?" I ask, changing the subject.

She tenses and looks at her hands in her lap. "Fine."

So help me if she says that word again, I'm going to kill her.

"Liar."

Her head snaps up and sadness flickers in her brown eyes. "I feel great right now. That's not a lie, Dr. Dan."

She uncrosses her legs only to cross them again. My eyes are drawn to the action, only maddening me further. Her fingertips toy with the hem of her dress. I can't tear my eyes from her smooth thighs and my dick is thickening, which is an annoying problem in these scrubs. As though she can see right into my head, her brown eyes skim lazily over me from head to toe. She pauses at my crotch area, a small smile tugging at her lips.

"Don't worry," she tells me as she stands. "I'll keep my virginity intact."

Fucking hell.

I step toward her and brush my thumb along the pink flesh of her skin. "Keep this clean and the pink will fade after a few months." I linger with my thumb running along her forehead, unable to let her go.

Her fingers flutter over the front of my chest, making me groan in response. "Any other doctor's orders?"

"Yeah," I grumble, "don't go on this date with Rex."

She smiles wide. "And why not?"

"Because I said so." My palm slides to the side of her throat and I check her pulse. "You should rest." I pull my hand back before I do something stupid like slide it down further to her breasts. "I have other patients to see."

Disappointment floods her features and I hate that I put it there.

"Here's to hoping I don't ever see you again," I tell her like the asshole I am.

It's the truth, though.

I don't want this beautiful, sassy woman to be hurting or sick. And every time I see her, I can't help but get the sense that something truly is wrong. Something she won't allow me to look into.

My phone buzzes with a text from my daughter, jerking me from the past.

Jenna: Enzo and I are going to see Cora at Patty's. Talk soon.

I smile as I reread the text. Jenna is in the process of trying to adopt her old foster sister. I'm proud of her. Anyone can see those two are meant to be together. I'm just happy I have Jenna in my life to be able to help her in any way I can. I've tried to make up for lost time by giving her my attention, buying her the things she needs, and simply being there for her when she needs to talk. As much as I want to rewind time to her birth and raise her with as much love as I can, life doesn't work that way. I got my daughter, but she was already a grown-ass woman with her own agendas. All I can do is allow her the space she needs to make her own life decisions without me meddling.

Now that I know I'm alone, I relax as I continue my task. Stalking Lauren Englewood. Her IG is full of lies too. She takes a lot of pictures of food, books, and sunsets. Most girls take selfies or have pictures with their friends or boyfriends. Lauren is closed off. I scroll all the way back to the beginning of her profile and find a picture of her and her mother. The caption is from Mother's Day a couple years ago and says, "Always thinking about you."

Poor girl.

Her mother is dead, her brother is a typical dumbass high school boy, and her dad is absent from what I can tell. It makes me wonder if she's lonely. The urge to message her privately is strong, but I don't want to get my ass in trouble in case she doesn't want to hear from me. With social media, you can't do stupid shit like leave trails of your unethical behavior. And messaging my patient to check on her isn't ethical.

My phone buzzes again.

Morris: I'll be late to the gym. See you soon.

I let out a heavy breath, closing out of IG, and set to getting dressed in my gym clothes so I can go expel some steam. Twenty minutes later and I'm trotting into the gym with my bag slung over my shoulder. I find my way over to the weights and drop my bag. I'm on my second set of curls when Morris graces me with his presence.

"You smell like pussy," I groan as soon as he joins me.

He smirks. "Chrissy's clinginess comes in handy when I need to get laid."

"You're an asshole."

"Proudly."

I smirk at him and then lie down on the bench. He sets his bag down and walks over to spot me.

"You seem edgy today and quiet. What's up?" he asks.

Gripping the bar, I shrug before lifting. "Just thinking about shit."

We take turns a few sets, spotting each other, until my muscles are burning and I'm soaked in sweat. I kneel to wipe my face on a rag when Morris lets out a groan.

"Jesus," he hisses. "If I didn't already smell like pussy, I'd be all over trying to hit that."

I follow his stare to a nice ass in black spandex. The woman's blond hair is pulled back in a ponytail that swings as she talks to what must be her boyfriend. When she feels our stare, she turns to look our way.

Holy shit.

"Lauren?"

"You know her?" Morris mutters. "Introduce us."

I stand quickly and throw my towel down forcefully. "No. She's mine."

"You're dating that young thing? No fucking way, man!"

"What? No. I'm not...forget it. Just stay here."

He laughs after me as I stride over to Lauren.

Her brown eyes slide over my body in a greedy way that makes my blood heat and my cock swell. This girl is bad news for me. I react way too much in her presence.

"Daniel," she says, her naturally pink lips quirking on one side.

"Lauren."

Her boyfriend comes to stand behind her, but when our eyes meet, I realize based on the same eyes boring into me this is her brother whom I'd met a couple times before.

"Can we talk?" I ask her, needing to get away from his scrutinizing gaze.

"Uh, yeah. Landon, I'll meet you over at the elliptical machines in a minute."

As soon as he's gone, I reach forward and touch the pale pink line on her forehead. She doesn't flinch under my touch.

"How are you feeling?"

"We're not at the hospital," she says. "You don't get to play doctor right now."

But she doesn't move away from my touch. Her skin is paler than when I saw her last. Brows slightly pinched. It makes me wonder if she's in pain.

"I've been worried about you," I admit, dropping my hand and fisting it. I don't tell her that an hour ago I was stalking her on social media.

"I'm f—"

I press my thumb to her lips. "Don't say it."

Her brown eyes flash with defiance.

"Hi, I'm Evan."

I tense when Morris comes to stand beside me and I reluctantly drop my hand from Lauren's supple lips. She pulls her stare from mine to flicker over to him. Her eyes dance up to his hair and she smiles. Of course. They all smile over Mr. Pretty Boy's hair.

"Pleasure to meet you. I don't often meet Daniel's girlfriends."

Her skin floods crimson. "What?"

"Morris," I grumble. "Come on, man."

A chuckle rumbles from him. "My mistake. When you'd said she was yours, I assumed—"

I let out an annoyed growl and give him a shove. The fucker just laughs harder.

"My bad," he says. "Nice to meet you…"

"Lauren." Her eyes leave him and she burns me with a glare.

"Right, so I'm going to go take a piss. Meet you back over by the weights in a minute." He bounces off and my tension leaves with him.

"Yours?" she implores.

I run my fingers through my sweaty hair and grit my teeth. "He's a player. If I didn't claim you, he'd already have your number and you'd fall into his sex trap."

She snorts. "Sex trap? Sounds kinky."

"Virgin girls don't belong in sex traps. I was protecting you."

"So noble," she taunts. "And here I thought it was because you wanted me all for yourself."

I'm about to retreat and leave her before I do something idiotic like kiss her, when she makes a strange sound. She sways and frantically grips the front of my soaked shirt.

"I need air," she whispers against my neck.

Curling my arm around her, I guide her out the side door and into the warm April late evening. There's nowhere to sit, so I walk her over to a shady area and help her sit down on the concrete. She crosses her legs, and with her elbows on her knees, she buries her face in her palms. I kneel beside her and stroke my fingers through her ponytail.

"Talk to me," I say gently. "I can't help you unless you talk to me."

Her shoulders shake as she cries silently. Anxiety ripples through me.

"Can we just sit and watch the sunset?" she whispers.

"Are you going to faint or become sick?"

"I'm better already."

"I'll do it on one condition."

She lifts her head and stares at me wearily. I reach forward and brush away a rogue tear with my thumb.

"What's the condition?" she asks.

"You call me the next time you feel sick."

Her nostrils flare. "I'll watch the sunset alone."

Grumbling, I sit down on my ass beside her. "Are you always this fucking stubborn?"

"Always," she sasses, flashing me a pretty smile that no doubt gets her out of lots of trouble.

"No one should have to watch a sunset alone," I grunt out. "And no one should suffer through something by themselves. All I'm asking is for you to talk to me. As a friend, not as a doctor."

Her body relaxes as she leans her head against my shoulder. "Fine."

This time, I like the word. I like it a lot.

CHAPTER
four

Lauren

Oranges and pinks light up the sky as night chases the sun into hiding. My world calms as I watch the sunset. It's the one thing that reminds me most of Mom. We'd sit on the back porch and watch it together. Dad and Landon don't have the patience for it. Now that she's gone, I haven't watched one with anyone. Sitting with Daniel feels right and peaceful.

"It's okay to let people help you," he says softly. "I want to help you."

Pain cuts through my chest and I suppress a sob. "I thought it'd go away."

His hand finds mine and we thread our fingers together. It feels anything but friendly or doctorly, but the connection warms me, so I cling to his hold on me.

"Thought what would go away?" he asks, brushing his thumb over my hand. "Tell me."

"The constant pain. The headaches. The blood."

"Blood?"

I tremble as I shrug. "Yeah."

"In your urine?"

Oh geez. It's easy to forget he's an ER doctor when he's sweaty, holding my hand, and watching a sunset with me.

"Yep."

He pulls away slightly to burn his intense green eyes into me. "Lauren, you need to see a doctor about this."

I let out a harsh laugh. "Looking at one right now."

He flashes me a crooked grin. "Smartass."

"Better than being a dumbass," I argue with a smile of my own.

I'll take playful banter over serious health talks any day of the week.

"Will you make an appointment to see your physician? Please?"

"Yeah," I utter. "I guess."

"Good," he says, letting out a harsh breath of relief. "We'll exchange numbers and I can check up on you. I'd feel better about that."

My eyes drop to his full lips, lingering for a long moment before finding his eyes again. "Were you serious about just being there to talk?"

He leans forward, and for a split second, my heart leaps hoping he'll kiss me. Instead, he rests his forehead to mine. "Absolutely. We'll go back inside and exchange numbers. Maybe even meet up for dinner one day to catch up."

I smile. "Sounds an awful lot like a date, Dr. Dan."

"Maybe we ought to get your ears checked too," he teases.

I swat at him and he laughs.

We missed the sunset, but I don't mind. Staring at Daniel's handsome face is pretty nice too.

I suck down a water bottle, but my stomach is killing me. I'm afraid to read up on it on the Internet, so I settle for period pains. Yep, definitely period pains. Too bad I had my period last week.

It's been two days since I saw Daniel at the gym, and he's checked on me via text each day. I haven't reached out to him yet. Something in me implores me to do so.

Me: Whatcha doin', Dr. Dan?

He doesn't respond and it makes me wonder if he's at work. I writhe around on the bed until the urge to pee hits me hard. Groaning, I climb out of bed and stumble to the bathroom. I sit down on the toilet, but the pee doesn't come. Everything aches and when I finally manage to pee, it feels like a horrible effort. The water clouds with pink, indicating more blood.

Shit. Shit. Shit.

A whimper claws up my throat.

Denial is getting me nowhere.

After wiping and washing my hands, I text Daniel again.

Me: Definitely blood in my urine. Everything hurts.

Fifteen minutes later, my phone buzzes.

Daniel: I'm at work so I missed your texts. Have your brother bring you in.

Me: He's not here. Movies with Callie.

Daniel: Your dad?

Me: Houston for work.

Daniel: Give me your address.

I stare at the text, shaking my head.

Me: I am not going in another ambulance. I'm fine.

Daniel: So help me, Lauren, next time you use that word, I'm going to spank you. Give me your damn address so I can come get you.

Holy shit, he's pissed.

With a heavy, resigned sigh, I shoot him my address.

I wake to fingers on my throat, confused at how much time has passed. I must have fallen asleep after texting him.

"Shh. Lie still. I'm checking your pulse," Daniel says softly, perched on the bed beside me.

I squint at him. Tonight he's not in scrubs. He's

wearing a white lab coat over slacks, a white dress shirt, and a green tie. Dang, he looks hot.

"Your pulse is erratic," he murmurs.

"Not my fault you came in looking like a damn snack."

He doesn't laugh at my joke. He's too busy frowning in concerned doctor mode.

"How did your mother die?" he asks abruptly as though the question doesn't rattle me to my core.

"What?"

"You heard me."

I roll away from him, pulling my pillow to my face. Hot tears flood my eyes and soak the pillow. The bed sinks and his warm body envelops mine. Strong fingers stroke through my hair in a gentle, comforting way.

"Let me help you, honey."

Honey.

My heart flutters at the name.

Releasing the pillow, I roll onto my back. Our eyes meet, intense and heated. He runs his fingertip along my cheek and sighs.

"Please, Lauren."

Tears prickle my eyes again. My bottom lip wobbles as the pain inside my heart begs for release. But the pain of losing your mother can't be unleashed into the wild. No, it stays caged. Punished and abused.

"Kidney failure. She had kidney disease."

His features grow stormy. "Jesus fucking Christ. Why didn't you tell me sooner?"

A sob chokes my throat. "B-Because saying my fears makes them true. I c-can't let this be true."

He leans forward and brushes his lips across mine in the softest of kisses. "We're going to the hospital and you're going to let me help you. No more hiding."

Hot tears leak from my eyes. "I'm scared."

"Me too," he admits, vulnerability on his handsome face making him seem decades younger. "But I'm going to fix you. Trust me."

The doctors couldn't fix Mom.

But when his lips press to mine more firmly, I can't help but stupidly allow hope to flood through me. I part my lips and he takes the invitation to swipe his tongue across mine.

Minty.

Yum.

His palm is strong and powerful as he cradles my cheek. Our lips move eagerly together, while our tongues thrash against one another. When a low groan of need pulses through me, Daniel pulls abruptly away.

"I shouldn't have kissed you," he whispers, his eyes betraying his words as they linger at my swollen lips. "It's not right."

"Felt pretty right to me," I argue.

He scrubs his face with his palm. "I'm your doctor."

Rolling my eyes, I try to pull him to me for another kiss, but he breaks away. "Come on. Let's get you to the hospital."

Rejection stings, but the pain searing through my abdomen is worse. It's the only reason I allow him to pull me up and to take me to get the dreaded tests. Something tells me things will get worse before they get better. And there's no more denying that fact.

Daniel falls into doctor mode easily now that I've given him a bone to chase after. While I sit in the hospital bed, anxiously awaiting the results of many tests he ordered, I can't help but be angry at myself for agreeing to this. When he was in my bed looking good enough to eat, I would've agreed to anything to get him to stay there. It's easy to forget outside of the hospital who he is. But in this sterile bed, I'm quickly reminded of who I've recently befriended.

Friends.

Yeah, right.

When I'd seen him at the gym looking sweaty and all his muscles were on glorious display, I'd wanted anything but friendship. I wanted him to strip me down right then and fuck me into the rubber mats as he greedily stole my virginity. But I'd let my secret slip and now I'm nothing more than a problem to be solved.

"We should call your dad," he says, his voice firm as he reenters the room.

"No," I snip. "He's working."

Daniel's features tighten. "I don't give a damn if he's working. This is important, Lauren."

I shrug, fighting tears in my eyes. "I guess."

He stalks over to me and gently grips my jaw. "Stop."

"Stop what?"

"Stop it with the walls."

A tear slips from my eye, racing down my cheek. "Am I going to die?"

My words make him flinch and he releases me. "Not if I can help it."

"Not comforting, Dr. Dan."

He sits on the edge of the bed and grips my hand. "I won't sugarcoat it, honey. Your blood-work and urinalysis came back. Not good. Kidney infection."

I wince at his words.

"I want to send you in for an ultrasound of your kidneys. The ultrasound will give us a better picture."

The curtain opens and he tugs his hand from mine to greet the nurse I now know as Lin. Daniel stands so that she can do her job of starting an IV.

"Antibiotics," he explains. "I will want to keep you overnight so we can make sure the antibiotics are working. But here shortly, I want them to do an ultrasound on your kidneys so we can rule out any-thing terrible." He lets out a heavy sigh. "Please call your dad."

I grit my teeth. "Do what you have to do. I'll text Dad later." Later as in I'll talk to him when he gets home next week.

Daniel scowls at me, clearly onto my lies. "Fine."

"Fine," I bite back.

But nothing is fine.

CHAPTER
five

Daniel

Of course the day I finally get her to agree to tests, triage is a fucking nightmare. I've put in the order for an ultrasound, but she's on a list behind sixteen other people. With each patient I see, I'm distracted with worry. Hours fly by and when I peek into her room, she's gone.

Finally.

I'm assessing a kid's wrist to see if he broke it when Lin taps me on the shoulder.

"Ummm, Dr. Venable?"

"Yep," I say, not looking up at her.

"She left."

This grabs my attention. I snap my head up. "What?"

"Lauren left."

I grit my teeth through the rest of my assessment before ordering an X-ray. Then, I storm over to find Lin at the nurse's station.

"Who cleared her to leave?" I growl.

She holds up both palms in defense. "Her dad

showed up. Dr. Wilkins went to meet with him when her father started throwing a fit. Wilkins prescribed her antibiotics and discharged her."

"Before or after the ultrasound?"

"Before. She would've still been waiting for that at least two more hours."

I run my fingers through my hair and then pull out my phone.

Me: You left? Really?

She responds immediately.

Lauren: It's technically the next day. I stayed overnight. I'm going to make an appointment with my doctor tomorrow.

Me: That was really stupid. You're sick.

Lauren: Fuck you too.

With a huff of frustration, I stuff my phone back in my pocket. "Where's my next patient?"

Lin points to triage six and I storm away. There's no point in getting pissy now. She's gone and my shift won't be over for a few more hours.

❧

Two weeks later…

"You should have bought my car from me. It's time for an upgrade," Morris taunts, driving me up a fucking wall.

"My daughter doesn't need your sex trap car." I

give him a pointed look. "She'd get pregnant just sitting in it."

"She's already pregnant and that had nothing to do with me." He snorts. "If I didn't think that new husband of hers wouldn't gut me, I'd try to get her in my car just to piss you off."

"*I'll* gut you with the pen in your pocket, motherfucker. Me. Not Enzo. Your superior."

The asshole laughs so hard he chokes.

I'm not as amused. I've got a lot of shit on my mind lately. Jenna recently decided to commit a felony, get pregnant, and get married all in the span of a few weeks. To top that off, I'm trying my hand at fostering. All for my daughter. I'd do anything for her. And I'll continue to do so.

But that's a story for another day...

Today, my mind is pulled in one direction.

Lauren.

I know I pissed her off when we texted a couple of weeks ago because she's since stopped responding. Now that I've cooled off, my anger is replaced by worry. I'm off tonight, so I'll go try and talk to her in person.

My phone buzzes, but I can't answer it because triage goes wild with activity. A city bus side swiped a row of cars and now we have people piling into the ER with various injuries. Morris and I fall into action, treating everything from scrapes on the head from hitting the window to possible broken necks.

Hours go by and my phone rings a few more times. When my shift ends, I check my phone to see Mom's been trying to get ahold of me. I slip into the break room and dial her back.

"Hey," I say in greeting. "Everything okay?"

"I'd be happier if you'd answer your phone the first time."

"I'm at work, Mother."

"You must have been dealing with that accident that was all over the news, hmm?"

"Yep." I scrub my palm over my face. "What do you need?"

"I wanted you to confirm that you and Jenna will be over on Sunday."

"Sunday?"

A sigh of exasperation rattles through the line. "I'll allow you a moment to think, son."

"Mom…" I'm really fucking tired and don't have time for this shit.

"It's Mother's Day," she huffs. "You asked Jenna, right?"

Well, fuck.

"I forgot, but I will. I'm sorry."

"You're normally my extremely responsible son, so I'll forgive you this time." She chuckles. "Hopefully your shift ends soon so you can get some rest. You clearly need it."

"I'll be there whether Jenna can make it or not. Should I bring anything?"

"A daughter-in-law would be nice."

Here we go. "Mom…"

"I'm teasing."

She's not.

"Right. I'll see you Sunday. Love you," I say quickly and hang up before she can take me on another guilt trip.

I text Jenna before I forget.

Me: Hey, sweetheart. Your grandma wants us over Sunday for Mother's Day.

Her response is immediate.

Jenna: Oh darn! I didn't realize we had plans, so I told Enzo I'd go with him to eat with his parents. I'm sorry.

Me: No worries. I'll let her know. Love you.

Jenna: Love you too, Dad.

My heart swells. Every time I hear "Dad," it blows my mind. I'm a father and will soon be a grandfather in less than a year's time. Funny how life can change in the blink of an eye.

I haven't tried to text Lauren in a couple of days because I've been busy as hell, so I decide now's a better time than any. I don't expect a response.

Me: How did your appointment go?

Lauren: Fine.

Rather than firing off a million questions like I want, I head out of the chaos to my midnight black Audi R8 coupe. Sure, Morris has the awesome ass Porsche, but my Audi will always be my baby. I loved it so much, I got Jenna one too. Hers has two more doors than mine. She's going to need them.

The sun is dipping close to the horizon by the time I reach Lauren's house. Her dad has money, though I still don't know what he does for a living. I'm not particularly looking forward to meeting the guy, because frankly I'd like to throttle him for ignoring his daughter's health needs. I park in the driveway and walk to the front door. After ten minutes of knocking and not being answered, worry niggles at me. But then I hear laughter. Sweet and melodic. Backyard.

I'm totally a creep, but I don't care as I stalk around the side of the house and through the gate. I find Lauren on the phone as she bends over, situating something on the porch floor.

"Love you too." Another laugh. "Bye, Dad."

She hangs up and then positions her phone as though she's taking a picture of what's at her feet. I take a moment to assess her health—because clearly that's the reason I run my greedy eyes up her bare, tanned legs. She's barefoot and wearing jean shorts with frayed ends. They're short enough that the pockets stick out beneath the denim. Her black Rolling Stones shirt is fitted, nicely hugging her breasts. It's her hair, though, that I have such an intense craving to touch. Long, golden, blond. It hangs halfway down her back in messy waves.

She's beautiful.

I kissed her a couple of weeks ago like she was mine.

And then…

She left.

Hurt burns inside my gut, but I ignore it. My dumbass hasn't dated in so long I can't even remember how to be normal. I should be after women my age, not one who just graduated with my daughter. I'm twenty-seven years her senior, which is kind of fucked up.

Maybe the kiss was unwanted.

What young woman would want her old doctor trying to make out with her?

Then that means I misread our chemistry and her expressions and our touches. Goddammit.

"You going to keep standing there looking like a psycho muttering to yourself or are you going to watch the sunset with me?"

The sassiness in her voice jerks my attention to her. She has one hand on her hip with it cocked out to the side. A dark blond brow is arched high in challenge and she's smirking. It makes me want to suck that half smile, half sneer right off her juicy lips.

No.

I need to erase those thoughts.

She's eight-fucking-teen.

I clear my throat and shrug. "I guess."

Her brown eyes gleam with victory as she turns and walks over to the porch swing. My gaze follows her ass in her tight denim shorts. She looks healthy and hot as hell. I follow her, unbuttoning my dress shirt at my wrists and rolling up my sleeves. It's warm and watching her makes it that much hotter.

We sit on the swing together. She turns her body to face mine, boldly stretching her legs across my lap. Fuck, she confuses the hell out of me. Like the greedy bastard I am, I slide my palm up her lower leg from her ankle to her knee and then back again. Goose bumps rise on her flesh at my touch.

"Why are you here, Dr. Dan? To take my rectal temperature?"

I grit my teeth and shoot her a warning glare. "Stop."

"Why would I want to stop when going is so much more fun?" She laughs, but I don't laugh back. "Aww," she croons. "Come on. Don't be like that. I missed you."

This gets my attention.

I study her features closely. Despite her smile and sunny disposition, worry and fatigue claim her. Her brown eyes are intense and her brows slightly pinched. The dark circles under her eyes lead me to believe she's not getting much rest. I run my palm back up her thigh, hoping to comfort her. She relaxes and leans her shoulder on the back of the swing before her gaze drifts beyond the porch to the setting sun. I sense that she wants peace, so I follow her stare and watch it go down. My hand slides up and down her leg, never stopping.

"What's all that?" I ask, pointing to the flowers and books and plate of cookies on the porch floor.

She smiles. "I was working on something for my blog.

"You have a blog?"

"Keep up, stalker."

Slipping my hand to her foot, I give the bottom a tickle. "Are you always such a smartass?"

She laughs and tries to pull her foot away, but I grip it to keep her from going anywhere.

"When I'm feeling great, I am."

This should calm my erratic heart, but it doesn't.

"You're feeling great right now?"

"I feel better than I have in months."

A huge "but" lingers in the air.

"But what?" I can't help but ask. I need to know.

She shrugs. "Why are you here?"

Because I'm fucking obsessed with you.

"To check on you," I grumble.

"Your bedside manner is commendable," she teases. "Maybe I should interview you for my blog."

I tickle her foot again. "And what questions would you ask?"

My words interest her because she meets my stare and toys with my tie, a beautiful smile on her face. "I'd ask you what's your favorite part of being a doctor."

"Helping people."

"Generic. Give me something juicy and good."

"I like fixing people in their most traumatic times and giving them hope when they may not have had any coming in."

"Right, so this is going to be harder than I thought. My blog followers like the nitty gritty. Your hero answers aren't working." But despite her words, she likes my answer based on her cute smile. "Okay, so what do you eat when you're slammed busy at the ER?"

"Usually I grab a Mountain Dew and a package of those little vanilla cookies. The sugar keeps me going."

"And how do you keep those abs of steel with that kind of diet, Dr. Dan?"

"I'm a gym nut. So sue me."

"Oh, definitely not punishing you for that one." She grins wickedly at me. "Maybe I should take a picture of those abs. My blog would definitely like that."

"Next question." I playfully grumble but wink at her.

"Hmm, so how come you're not married?"

Maybe Mom will subscribe to this blog. It's her favorite question.

"I haven't found the one," I mutter. "I don't date much."

"Why not?"

"Women don't like men who are married to their careers."

Her brows furrow. "But you love your job."

"Women want to be loved more."

"You can love both."

"I know I could, but try telling that to the women I've dated over the years."

Her lips purse together. "Those women are bitches."

I laugh because she has a point.

CHAPTER
six

Lauren

I'd been mad. Infuriated even. Two weeks ago, Daniel dragged me to the ER with good intentions, but then he fell into obsessed doctor mode, hunting for answers. The connection I'd felt to him—especially after our kiss—was severed as I lay in that bed stewing over my ailments. When Dad showed up, I was more than ready to bail. And with a little urging, I was able to get Dad to make that happen.

All Daniel's texts and calls were easy to ignore. I felt great with the antibiotics and was getting over my kidney infection. I'd even felt good enough to do a long overdue blog post.

And then he showed up.

Our connection hadn't been cut. If anything, it was stronger. He tugged on the invisible cord as soon as we made eye contact. I willingly fell into his presence. Now, as he strokes my leg as though it's the most natural thing for him to do, I realize how wrong I was.

We like each other.

It's clear as day in the way we banter and our proximity.

The urge to kiss him again is strong. I've never dated an older man. He's older than Dad by six years. I know this because I looked Daniel Venable up on social media. We may have not spoken for two weeks, but I've spent my lonely, depressed times checking in on him.

Oranges and pinks in the sky have faded to dusty purples and now dark blues. The sun is gone and I can hear the crickets chirping as the evening rolls in.

"I missed you," Daniel mutters, his palm lingering above my knee on my inner thigh. "I thought about you more than what was probably necessary."

He seems embarrassed by his words.

"Lauren..."

"Hmmm?"

"This thing going on between us...it's more than a doctor caring about his patient. Tell me it's not one-sided. I haven't dated much, so I feel out of the loop on reading people like I should. I'll feel like a fucking bastard if I'm pursuing you and you don't want it." Shame coats his words as he starts to pull his hand away from my thigh.

I grip his wrist and shake my head. "Don't you dare pull your hand away, Dr. Dan. I quite like your obsessive tendencies when it comes to my well-being."

He snorts. "You're a brat."

"Your brat," I amend, smiling.

"Mine, huh?"

"If you want me." My voice is meant to come out sassy, but even I can hear the vulnerability in it. With Dad working all the time and Landon always gone, I'm alone far too much for my liking. With Daniel, I feel alive, on fire, and tethered to the moment.

"Of course I want you," he murmurs, squeezing my thigh. "I wouldn't be here if I didn't."

I sit up and boldly straddle his lap on the swing. Sweat trickles down my spine as I worry he might push me away. His face is stony and serious. He clenches his jaw as I try to calm my erratic heartbeat. Sitting on his thighs with my hands on his shoulders feels natural. When I lick my lips in a nervous way, he finally slides his palms to my ass, gently squeezing. Emboldened by his touch, I lean forward and press my lips to his. The kiss is sweet and simple until we both part our lips. He meets the urgency of my tongue with his own. His hands grip my ass tighter this time, urging me closer. As soon as I rub against his dick through his slacks, I let out a breathy moan.

"Christ," he hisses, nipping at my bottom lip. "Do you have any idea what you do to me?"

I smile against his mouth, rocking my hips, hoping to bring him pleasure with my own body. His breath is hot and the groans coming from him are so male and erotic it makes my head spin. One of his palms works its way under my shirt, caressing my lower back. I'm sweaty there and it makes me still, embarrassed.

"Is this okay?" he asks, his voice rough.

"I'm sweating," I mutter.

He chuckles. "It's 'cause you're so hot."

"You're supposed to save the dad jokes for your kid, not your girlfriend."

Pulling away slightly, he lifts a brow at me. "Girlfriend?" In the dark, I can barely make out his features, but he's amused, not annoyed.

"It sounds a lot better than 'the girl you stalk.' Am I right?"

He leans forward and nips at my chin.

"Hey!" I say with a laugh. "You just bit my chin. That's so weird."

His lips press kisses to the spot he just bit. "Told you I've been out of the game awhile. Certainly never had a 'hot girlfriend' before."

"You're a dick."

"And you're a brat a lot of the time. I'd say we're evenly matched."

This time when he bites me, it's on my neck. He distracts me with his mouth as his palm caresses my lower back. Shivers, despite the warm summer air, ripple through me.

"Have you eaten dinner?" he asks, pulling back.

"Are you asking as my boyfriend or my doctor?"

"Does the answer vary based on which one?"

"It depends on whether or not I'll send you home."

"You're a brat," he grumbles. "I can say that because apparently I'm your boyfriend now."

"Good." I tug on his tie. "I haven't eaten. Want me to cook something for you?"

His brows lift in surprise. "You know how to cook?"

A wave of sadness washes over me. "My mom loved to cook. We spent a lot of time hanging out in the kitchen together."

He starts to say something, but then stops himself before patting my ass. "Let's get in there so you can show me your skills. I'm hungry as hell. It's been a wild day at the ER."

Reluctantly, I slide out of his lap and stand. I'd much rather sit in his lap and make out, but the mosquitos are nearly as hungry as I am.

"Any allergies?"

"None."

"I'm thinking spaghetti. It's pretty quick and my mom's recipe is the best you've ever had."

He chuckles as he stands. "Don't tell my mom that."

∽

While I boiled noodles and browned hamburger meat, Daniel ran out to his car to grab his bag. He changed out of his fancy doctor clothes into a pair of jeans and black T-shirt. No matter what he wears, he's hot. Like now, as he hovers, inhaling the sauce smell as it simmers, I can't help but check out the way his shirt clings to his sculpted body.

"I'm dying," he rumbles, his hand patting my ass in a familiar way. "And this food smells so damn good."

"You act like you've never had a home-cooked meal before," I tease.

He shrugs. "I get them when Mom cooks. Jenna's not much of a cook, but her husband is. They're both so busy, though, so they eat out a lot."

"And you?"

"Whatever I can grab on the way to and from work."

I turn away from the stove and look up at him. Sure, he's older than me by a lot, but right now he seems so young. Like a college guy completely transfixed that his girlfriend knows how to cook.

"I'll cook for you anytime you want," I promise.

This earns me a wide grin. "Man, I should have gotten a hot girlfriend who cooks a long time ago. A guy could get spoiled."

I stand on my toes to brush a kiss over his lips before turning back to the food. He explores the kitchen, opening cabinets and fetching plates. All of this feels so comfortable and domestic. Truth is, Daniel is just easy to be around. I like his attention and his presence. He's funny and sexy and sweet.

Dad is going to die.

It's a buzzkill thinking about how Dad will take the knowledge that I'm so into my doctor. Knowing Dad, he'll try to be the present parent he's not and throw a damn tantrum. Landon, the carbon copy of Dad, will take his side and try to make me feel bad for being with Daniel.

I don't, though.

He's different than any guy I've dated.

Smarter. Cuter. Nicer.

My body catches fire when I look at him. I steal glances at him as I finish up cooking our dinner. Once I serve our plates and we sit down, I can't help but peek up at him. He wastes no time diving in. A groan rumbles from him and his wide eyes find mine. There's sauce on the corner of his lips. He swipes it with his thumb and then licks it off before grinning.

"You were right," he says.

"Aren't I always?"

He rolls his eyes. "It's pretty much the only thing you've ever been right about."

I playfully scoff. "Asshole. What was I right about?"

"Your spaghetti sauce is better than Mom's. Don't tell her I said that, though. I'll deny it until the day I die."

I pick up my fork and grin at him. "Thanks. But if you ever make me mad, I'll totally tattle on you."

His green eyes gleam with mischief as we eat.

The sauce is good, but it reminds me of Mom. This will be the second Mother's Day without her. That first one I barely crawled out of bed. This one, I can't imagine it'll be that much better, especially without Dad and Landon here.

"What's wrong?" Daniel's voice is gentle and his brows are scrunched together in concern. God, he's beautiful.

"Nothing," I say in a playful tone, but it falls flat.

He sees right through my façade. "Tell me about nothing then, because I sense it's still something."

I poke at my noodles with my fork. "Sunday will be my second Mother's Day without her." Hot tears burn at my eyes, and I bite on my bottom lip to keep from crying.

His chair scrapes along the tile as he stands. In the next moment, he's kneeling beside me, taking my hand. "Oh, honey, I'm so sorry."

A tear streaks down my cheek and he reaches up to swipe it away with his thumb. My throat hurts from stifling a sob. Exhaustion weighs heavily on me.

"I think I'm done," I mutter, pushing my plate forward.

He rises to his feet and helps me to mine. When I'm pulled into his strong embrace, I relax against him. "Why don't you get ready for bed? I'll clean up in here and come tell you good night before I leave."

I nod, but it's not what I want.

I don't want him to leave at all.

While Daniel cleans up the kitchen, I take a quick shower. I'm embarrassed that I got upset and ruined what's essentially our first date. I can't help it, though. I miss my mom so much. After I brush out my wet hair, I'm feeling slightly dizzy from the hot shower. I wrap my towel around my body and then head into my room on a hunt for clothes. I'm stopped short to find Daniel sitting on the edge of my bed, his green eyes sharp and probing as he rakes his gaze down my body. A shiver ripples through me.

"Cold?"

"Nope." I smirk at him. "Hot actually."

"That's a given." He spreads his thighs a little, so I take his unspoken command to come stand between them. "You feeling okay?"

I groan and start to pull away, but his strong hands grip my hips over my towel.

"You can't expect me to never ask about your well-being, Lauren. Don't put that on me because I can't be that person." His thumbs stroke me as he tilts his head up. "I obviously really care about you. Give me that."

Releasing a heavy sigh, I run my fingers through his hair. "I just don't want this relationship to be based on you worrying over me all the time. I want us to have fun and feel each other."

"I want that too," he murmurs, sliding his palms

to my ass. "But I can't change who I am. I won't nag you about your health, but I sure as hell won't shy away from it."

"Fine," I clip out.

He grips my ass, pulling me closer. "Fine." His lips tug into a crooked smile that makes my stomach flip. "Now come give me a kiss."

I grip his shoulders and then straddle his lap, my knees resting on the bed. He's hard beneath me, like before, and I want to grind against him. With nothing on under the towel, though, I worry about getting his jeans wet from my arousal. He grips my neck in a gentle, yet possessive way, and pulls me closer so our lips touch. His hot tongue slides against the seam of my mouth, begging for entrance. I let out a breath of anticipation, accepting his unspoken request, so I can taste him again. The moment our tongues clash, heat zips down my spine like a lightning strike, zapping me straight in my core. A small moan murmurs through me as I kiss him in a needy way.

Where I kiss like I need his taste to live, he kisses me like he wants to devour every cell in my body. Consume or be consumed. In my case, he consumes me. Decimates me to my soul. Kisses me with a fire that's catching and cataclysmic.

"Lauren, baby, you're turning me into a madman," he growls against my mouth. "And I fucking love it."

I smile, but then he steals it with a bite to my

lip. A claim. A promise. A warning. He's the leader in our naughty parade. His hand slides to my hair, gripping it tight enough I'm unable to move. He tilts my head back, exposing my neck. Hot breath tickles my still-wet flesh just below my jaw line. His tongue slides out and he licks me. Firm, owning, powerful. Desire tingles through my every nerve ending. My towel has loosened enough that I'm able to grind my pussy along his obvious erection. He lets loose a grunt and nips at my throat.

For being a doctor, he's awfully feral and dangerous when he loses control. I love it. It makes me wonder if he'd suck me hard enough to leave bruises all over my skin. If he's the type of man who'd fuck you raw. Something tells me he'd be relentless and dominant in his lovemaking, but will still deliver pleasure. My towel slides down my breasts and pools at my hips.

"Uh-oh," he rasps, pulling away to admire my breasts. His green eyes flame bright with lust and he licks his lips. "Of course your tits would have to be perfect."

I laugh, making them jiggle. "You like them?"

"I love them," he growls, gripping them in his palms. His thumbs caress my nipples in a teasing way, making them firm up into hard peaks.

A thrill shivers through me. With his eyes lifted to mine, he leans down and tongues one of my nipples. I suck in a sharp gasp. Pleasure assaults me where his wet tongue teases me. His eyes leave mine when he covers his mouth over my breast. He kisses my tender flesh like he kisses my mouth. All I can do is moan and rock my hips along his hard cock through his jeans. He sucks on more than just my nipple. His large mouth seems to consume my entire breast. It's erotic watching him try to devour the whole damn thing. He pops off, leaving my breast soaked and aching. Then, he gives the other one the same attention. All I can do is wriggle my hips, seeking relief from the friction of his massive dick that's trying to rip through his jeans.

"I want to see all of you," he whispers before teasing my breast with a playful nip. He draws away from me as his hands grip my towel. A few tugs later and it's gone.

I'm naked.

Shaking and eager and hot.

Embarrassment should be washing over me right now, but it doesn't. I feel desired and wanted and craved. It emboldens me to rock my hips. Our eyes fall to my pussy—the way my pink lips part around the girth of his cock. His denim is streaked with my arousal.

"Oh, fuck, Lauren." His voice is a raspy growl. He slides his palms up my thighs and grips hard enough I wonder if I'll be bruised.

"What's wrong?"

"Nothing."

"You look angry," I tease.

His eyes, burning with desire, land on mine. "I am anything but angry right now. I'm horny as hell, baby. I want to flip you over on this bed and fuck away your virginity."

"So do it," I challenge.

He slides his hands farther up my legs. "I can't."

Shock ripples through me, making me stop my movements. "Why not?"

"Because I'm not fucking you tonight."

I gape at him. "I'm literally ready to be fucked and your dick is hard as stone. Why the hell not?"

He smirks—fucking smirks—at me. Cocky ass doctor.

"I don't fuck before the first date," he tells me, his fingers biting into my hips now, urging me to move.

"We just had a date," I bite out. My hips move under his guidance despite the fury raging inside me.

"No, baby, we had dinner. I'm taking you on a date. You're going to have fun. And then I'm going to take your virginity in my bed where I can keep you all night."

Oh.

Well, when he puts it that way.

"But what about right now?" I whine. "I need…" Truth is, I don't know what I need. Relief. Assurance. Tenderness.

"I know what you need, my beautiful girl," he rasps as he undoes the button on his jeans. "Take me out and feel me. I may not fuck you tonight, but I'm still going to give you something you need. We can still play."

"Maybe I don't want to play games," I lie.

He smirks. "But my games are fun, Lauren. Now take my dick out and feel how hard you make me."

Bossy fucker.

Apparently I like to be bossed around, though, because I unzip his jeans and push his boxers down so I can tug out his cock. Thick. Veiny. Long. It's intimidating as hell. I wonder what it would feel like inside me. Will he make me bleed?

"No fucking," he reminds me. "If you fuck me, you lose the game."

A challenge rises up inside me. "Oh, I don't lose."

"That's what I thought," he says with a grin. "Now do what feels good. Use me, baby."

His words light a fire inside me. I grip his shaft and jerk it slowly. I've given a few hand jobs before. To guys my age. Normal dicks. Daniel's dick is like the king of dicks. The crème de le crème. Big and powerful.

I want to rub against him.

If I can't have him in me, I want to feel him on me.

With my eyes locked on his, I scoot forward and continue what I was doing earlier, this time nothing between us. He hisses when my wet pussy slides along his shaft. Smooth and velvety. I groan in pleasure. It feels really good. His hands grip my ass and he urges my movement. Up, up, up until I could almost shift my body and take him inside of me, but then back down, down, down to the root of his cock where his trimmed hairs tickle me. Needing closer, I thread my fingers in his hair and kiss him. With each rub along his shaft, I feel my pleasure building. The constant sliding on my clit is driving me wild.

He lies back, pulling me with him. It's easier from this position and I take control, moving my hips with a rhythm we both like. Our breaths are ragged and we begin to moan in unison.

"God, you're so fucking perfect," he groans, his fingers biting into my ass cheeks and spreading them. This movement parts my pussy even more, making me grind harder on him. I'm slick and easily fuck the outside of his dick.

"I want you inside me," I whine.

"Here?" he murmurs against my mouth as his finger slides barely into my wet pussy from behind.

"Mmm," I whimper, undecided if I want to sink farther on his finger or keep rubbing my clit on his cock.

His finger pushes in deep and I gasp. "Let me fuck you with this while you make me come with that." To emphasize *that*, he thrusts his hips up, making my clit throb.

Our mouths meet again, this time more frenzied. He fucks me with his finger, deep and hard, in tandem with the way I rub against him. I can almost pretend we're fucking for real.

"Daniel…" Oh, God, I'm close.

"That's it, baby, come all over my finger. Or are you a greedy girl who needs two?"

He presses another finger into me, stretching me. It hurts a little, but I like it. I nod and suck on his bottom lip.

"Very greedy," I agree.

He thrusts his hips up, aiding in my effort to reach release. I'm soaked and needy. Another finger squeezes inside me with the other two and it's officially too much. Yet, he's much bigger than his three fingers. Maybe I was jumping the gun. I cry out at the sharp pain of him stretching me. The fullness is something I could get used to, though. I'm dying to feel him truly inside me.

"Oh, fuck, baby," he groans, "I'm…"

His cock twitches below me and cum starts jetting. It's hot and soaks down his shaft, giving me more lubricant. I rub harder until I'm spiraling with him. Colors prickle at my vision and my body detonates with pleasure. We ride the crazy wave of ecstasy through every spasm on my end and every drop of cum on his.

"You're going to be the death of me." He nips at my lip. "Sweet way to go."

I lift up as he slides his fingers out of me. Wincing, I peek at him under my lashes. My hips are still moving along his wet dick and I can't help but look down at the mess we've made. His clothes that he's still wearing are soaking wet and his dick is smeared with a little blood mixed in with my creamy trail of arousal.

"You made me bleed," I state, transfixed by the way it looks on his cock.

"It's a good thing I'm a doctor."

CHAPTER
seven

Daniel

Goddamn, she's so fucking pretty.

And young.

Vulnerable and innocent as they come.

I need to get her tucked into bed so I don't finish what I started and impale her with my cock. A man only has so much restraint. And I told her the truth. I want to take her out before we sleep together. Although, what we just did was as close to fucking as two people can get. Still, I want to show her she's worth more than an easy lay. I want every part of her, not just her body.

"Let's get you cleaned up," I say as I gently move her over to the bed.

She closes her legs and frowns at me. I give her a soft smile before rising and rushing into the bathroom. As soon as I see my reflection, I take pause. My dark hair is wrecked and my lips are red and swollen from kissing. Cum soaks my shirt and jeans. And my dick just flops around like it's ready for round two. Still mostly hard and soaked with our dirty deed.

Stepping up to the sink, I turn the water on and clean myself off the best I can before drying off and zipping that bad boy back up in my jeans.

I need to get a hold of myself before going back in there. Scrubbing my palm down my face, I let out a heavy sigh. God, I can smell her on my hands and it's so fucking sweet. I grab a rag and wet it with warm water before heading back in her room. She's right where I left her, her brows furrowed and her fuckable lips pouting out. Her flesh is red and raw anywhere I kissed and sucked. I love the trail of me I've left on her.

"Spread your legs," I command, sitting beside her.

She smirks but obeys.

I lick my lips, admiring her sweet cunt. The shit I want to do to her is deviant as hell. Her blond hair is clipped short, revealing her pink pussy lips and dark pink clit that peeks out between them. She's red and raw looking from all the rubbing. If I didn't think it'd lead to more, I'd lick away the redness.

Dabbing at her pussy gently, I murmur, "Take a bath tomorrow and soak."

"Is this coming from Dr. Dan or boyfriend Daniel?"

"Both," I grumble. "I want you to heal up some because this time tomorrow, I'm going to fuck you wild."

"Dirty doctor," she teases.

I chuckle. "Seriously, though. How do you feel?"

"A little sore…" She chews on her bottom lip. "Why did I bleed?"

I finish cleaning her and then toss the rag. "Because that's what little virgins do."

When I stand and cover her with the blanket, she frowns at me. "Where are you going?"

"Home."

"I want you to stay."

"If I stay, I'm going to test my already fraying restraint."

She swallows and nods, but her eyes flash with loneliness. Ahh, fuck.

"How about I stay with you until you fall asleep?" I suggest.

Her eyes light up. "I'd like that."

I turn off the lights and kick off my shoes before sliding into bed beside her. Wrapping my arm around her, I nuzzle her hair and kiss her neck.

"You ever feel like your world's been knocked off its axis?" I ask.

She nods. "Yeah. Like now?"

"Yeah, like now."

"Is it bad?" she asks, her voice small and unsure.

"Not for us," I murmur. "For us, it feels really good."

"But?"

"Who says there's a but?"

"There's always a but."

I find her mouth in the dark and kiss it. "Not with us."

"Where are you taking me on our date tomorrow?"

"It's a surprise."

She relaxes, seemingly happy at my words. When she drifts off to sleep, I linger. I kiss her face and inhale her sweet scent. And I wonder what the fuck kind of date will be perfect enough for a girl like her.

Lauren knocked me off my axis all right.

And I'm not looking to fix it either.

I want her. All of her. For us to spin and spin off course until we're in our own little realm of happiness. Relationships that start out hot, fast, and fiery should last forever, right? I certainly have never felt this way about anyone before. Or is it the quicker they catch fire, the quicker they die out?

Nothing's dying on my watch.

I'll stoke her inner flame over and over.

I don't care if any of this is reckless and fast.

She's mine.

I'm not letting her go.

∞

"So let me get this straight," Morris says, groaning as he lifts the bar full of weights up high. "You're going on a date. You? Dr. I Don't Do Relationships?"

He sets the bar down and looks at me in confusion.

"Yes, dumbass, and I need unique ideas that don't involve something messy in the backseat of a sports car."

He snorts. "Well, there goes 99 percent of my dates."

"I want to give her something unique. Something perfect."

"Yeah, okay, stalker. Why don't you take her to the police station and file a restraining order on yourself?"

"Fuck off," I grumble. "I'm being serious."

He sits up and wipes the sweat from his face with a towel. "I can tell. That's what freaks me out. You're never serious about anyone."

No one has ever measured up to Lauren. She's beautiful and sexy and funny and fiery.

"Right, so you're looking about three seconds from rushing a jewelry store to buy an engagement ring. Let's dial back the romantics here for a sec, Romeo. What does she like?"

I think about her Instagram account. She likes food, that's a given. And sunsets. Books, too.

"I'm going to invite her to Mom's on Sunday," I tell him.

"Oh, Jesus," he groans. "I've lost you. You're head over fucking heels for this woman. What's her name again? Do I know her?"

"Lauren," I grit out.

"Lauren as in the hot young blonde from the gym a couple of weeks ago?"

His description of her grates on my nerves. "Yeah."

"Dude, she's a fucking teenager."

"Eighteen," I growl. "Your point?"

He laughs at me. "I thought you were just into her because she had a nice ass in yoga pants, but I didn't actually think you were that into her. How did you two meet anyway? Please don't tell me through your daughter."

I rub at the tension on the back of my neck. "Don't talk about her ass or I'll throttle you. And I met her…" I shoot him a helpless look.

"Don't fucking say at BCH."

"She was my patient and—"

"Shhh," he hisses. "Are you trying to get slapped with a lawsuit and lose your license?"

"It's not like that," I bark out.

"Man, you're five seconds from fucking your damn patient and you're telling me it's not like that." He shakes his head. "Me, I expect this of me. I'm a little shit. But you? Mr. Responsible? I just don't get it. Why her?"

"I don't know," I snap, fury burning through me. "I just connected with her and it grows more intense by the day. I want her more than anything I've ever wanted in my entire life."

"She's eight-fucking-teen," he reminds me. "I get the whole mid-life crisis shit, hence my badass car, but seriously, man? What could you possibly have in common with a little girl?"

"Your sudden sense of morality today is fucking annoying," I snap. "Can you stop being me for five seconds and be you? I need advice on a date, not a stern talking to. I'm not breaking it off with her. She's mine and I can't let her go. Not now, not ever."

Morris blinks at me as though I have three heads. "You're in love with a girl you barely know and who's barely legal. Is the pussy that good?"

I grab the front of his T-shirt and yank him to me so our noses nearly touch. "Don't talk about her that way. She's not some fuck to get my rocks off. She…she deserves more than I could ever give her, but I want to try. Understand, buddy? I want to give her everything."

He lets out a resigned sigh and I release his shirt.

"Okay," he grumbles. "So you're pussywhipped. Not that I'm familiar with this territory, but I am familiar with spoiling women. Tell me what she likes."

We spend the next fifteen minutes with me explaining Lauren. Feisty, fiery Lauren. I skim over the part where she's had health scares and get to the parts that define her. Granted, I don't know tons, but we'll get there. I give him what I do know. The books. The blog. The food.

"Well, stalker, may I make a suggestion before I

give you some date ideas?" he asks, his eyes alight with amusement.

"Sure, asshole."

"Next time, instead of putting your tongue down her throat, ask more about her. You're giving me little to work with here."

"I'm going to learn everything there is to know about her," I assure him. "Now spill."

"You know Vaughn Young?"

"Professor at the university?"

"Yep. Anyway, he's a buddy of mine. His wife and…" He scratches his jaw as he seems to try and formulate his words. "Well, anyway, his wife and this kid Aiden, they opened up this awesome restaurant. Best steak in town. But if your girl likes desserts, this is definitely the place. Vale's a master baker."

"Okay, you got the food part. This could work. Any other ideas?"

"Well, the best part is, it has rooftop dining that overlooks downtown. I bet you could catch a killer sunset there."

"And books?" I ask hopefully.

"You're on your own there, buddy, but since it's downtown, I'm sure you can figure something out."

My mind begins to form a plan. "Thanks, man."

"At least tell me she's this into you, too."

"She is," I assure him. That much I know for sure.

"Good, because I'm going to give you a little word of warning."

I frown. "What?"

"Be ready for the looks."

"What looks?"

"I dated younger chicks for a spell there. Trust me, people look at you like you're sugar daddy trash. It's unnerving."

"It's not like that," I growl.

"I know that, but they don't. A rich guy driving a car like yours with a fucking teenager on his arm looks bad."

"I don't care what they think."

"Well, hopefully she doesn't either. But others will have opinions." He tilts his head and studies me. "What does your mom think? Her dad?"

I'm not worried about Mom, but Teddy could be a problem.

"I get along great with Enzo, who's considerably older than my daughter," I argue. "He's perfect for Jenna."

"Jenna's only been in your life for what? Three seconds? You hardly had a say so in who she dated, Daniel. You're lucky to just have her in your life. Even if you hated Enzo, you would've never said a thing."

Fucker has a point.

"Fine. I've been warned. Do I need to make reservations at this place?"

"Nah, I'll text Vaughn to let him know just in case they get busy. He'll make sure you have a table." He grips my shoulder. "For what it's worth, I hope it works out. If anyone deserves happiness, it's you."

CHAPTER
eight

Lauren

"I'm fine, Dad," I say as I fuss with my hair in the hallway mirror. "It's just a date."

I don't tell him with whom. Something tells me he may not like that I'm going off with Dr. Venable.

"What's that? A date?" my brother chirps, rounding the corner.

"Gotta go. Love you." I hang up on my dad and frown at my brother. "I didn't know you came home last night."

Landon yawns and scratches his bare chest. "Got home like an hour ago while you were in the shower. I'm going to a party with some friends tonight. Everyone from school will be there. One last get-together before everyone goes off to college. You and your date want to come? Callie is going to be there."

"Nah, I'm good," I tell him, my voice tight. Last party I was with him at was his party and I ended up in the emergency room. Hard pass.

"Suit yourself." He peers past me. "Damn. Your guy is loaded. Is that an Audi?"

I swat at him. "Go away."

"No," he argues. "I want to meet the guy and make sure he's not an asshole."

"You're an asshole and I do just fine. I've got this. Leave, Landon. I'm serious."

"Is he ugly? Why are you embarrassed?"

"I'm not embarrassed," I say in a shrill tone. "I just don't need you overseeing everything I do."

He squints. "He's getting out. How old is this guy?"

I shove his chest and then snag up my purse before rushing out of the house. Daniel has barely stepped out of his vehicle, before I crash into his arms, my lips finding his.

"My nosey brother is watching," I groan against our kiss. "Can we hurry and bail? You can meet him some other time."

He stiffens but gives me a slight nod. "Sure. Let's get out of here."

It isn't until we're inside the vehicle and leaving the neighborhood that I finally sigh in relief. I got a weird vibe about the whole thing. Not Daniel, because I really like him. More like I was worried what Landon would have to say.

I'm not ashamed.

I just don't want to deal with his overprotective brotherly crap or the fact he'd tattle to our dad.

"Everything okay?" Daniel asks, reaching over to give my thigh a squeeze. He leaves his hand on my thigh below the hem of my dress and caresses my soft skin.

"Yeah. I'm excited about our date."

He smirks at me, his eyes leaving the road for a moment to scan over my outfit. I'd chosen a summery white cotton sleeveless dress that dips low in the front and hits mid-thigh. It hugs me in all the right places. I wasn't sure how fancy of a place we would go to and wanted to be comfortable, so I paired it up with a trendy pair of cowgirl boots.

"You look beautiful," he murmurs, flashing me a smile.

Not hot or sexy or fuckable.

Beautiful.

Somehow that feels better than a comment guys my age would normally throw my way.

"Thank you. You look pretty handsome yourself."

He's wearing charcoal-gray slacks that fit nicely around his muscular thighs. And a white button-up shirt sans tie with his sleeves rolled up. My gaze skims over his toned forearms that reveal the sexy kind of veins men have. It makes me want to lick up and down each one. While he drives, I admire how his shirt is tight over his biceps and shoulders. Last night, I'd clutched onto those arms and shoulders as I rode my way to ecstasy. A thrill of heat burns through my nerve endings.

In his car, I'm overwhelmed by the scent of him. Masculine, expensive, clean. His car is in perfect condition, but when I see a car seat in the back, I frown.

"You have a kid?" I blurt out.

He hikes a brow up. "Yeah. Is that a problem?"

I frown. I don't think it's a problem. It just makes jealousy burn up inside me. Not for the kid, but for the woman he was with to get said kid.

"No," I utter. "Just wondering."

"Her name is Jenna Pruitt. Well, Tauber is her last name now. She went to school with you and is friends with your friend Winter."

He means the same Winter who brought me to the ER last March.

"We're not exactly friends," I state with a huff.

This earns me a frown. "She claimed to be your sister. I surely thought you two were close."

Guilt gnaws away at me. After that day, Winter has texted me a few times, trying to reach out. She's best friends with my brother's girlfriend, though, so it felt like a forced friendship on my brother's part. Regardless, I feel bad for blowing her off.

"I'm not really close with anyone," I say quietly, hating that I'm once again putting a damper on the mood. "Besides you, Dr. Dan."

"It's okay to have friends and people to lean on," he replies in a gentle tone. "I'm learning that myself."

"So the car seat belongs to your daughter's kid? This makes you a grandpa?" I can't help but giggle.

He playfully grabs my thigh. "Knock it off."

"Or what? Usually I'd insert some daddy joke about you spanking me, but something tells me I need to level up to more *mature* jokes, Gramps."

"It's for the little girl I'm hoping to foster."

This sobers me up. "A doctor and a foster dad. Did I hit the good guy jackpot?"

"I'm a bad guy where it counts," he says with a teasing lilt as his eyes rake up my body. "But yeah. To help my daughter."

"She wants to foster? She's young, though."

"In my world, I'm learning age is just a number to quantify time, not something that factors in experience, heartaches, or maturity."

I think about losing my mother to illness. How my entire mindset changed. The things my peers were worried about—shows, dating, sex, popularity—were all insignificant to my own thoughts. It makes me wonder if Jenna is like me. I didn't have any classes with her, but I knew of her. A quiet girl who bounced between foster homes. I'd felt sorry for her, but we were on two different social ladders. It wasn't until she started hanging out with Winter that she'd really even blipped on my radar.

"How did that come about? Jenna, I mean. She was a foster kid, too, huh?"

He lets out a sad sigh. "I never knew about her. The woman—her mother—I'd been with long ago never mentioned having a baby and nothing ever surfaced when she died. But when I looked at Jenna for the first time, I knew she was mine. It was a chance ER meeting, but it changed my life for the better."

Seems like this happens a lot for the good doctor. "Kind of like us?"

"Jenna let me in her life almost instantly. You, though, require a lot more work." He winks at me. "My daughter and a little girl named Cora have been inseparable since Cora was put into the foster system. Jenna wants to adopt her, and at the very least foster her so they can be together. Problem is, she's just not old enough or established or experienced."

My eyes prickle with tears as I glance back at the car seat. "You're doing this for her?"

"She's my daughter. I have to do everything in my power to make her happy. That's what dads do."

I take his hand and thread our fingers together before squeezing him. "I like you, Dr. Dan."

"I like you too, angel."

We end up chattering about other lighter topics as we make it into downtown. The traffic isn't too bad and he finds us a parking spot on the street down one of the busier avenues that's lined with shops and restaurants.

"You hungry yet?" he asks as we get out of the car.

"I can eat. It's up to you."

He looks up at the sky and seems to be mentally

calculating something. With a shake of his head, he points toward an old brick building. "Let's kill an hour or so in here and then we'll head to the restaurant."

I take his hand and allow him to guide the way. It feels right with our fingers linked together. Sure, I've been on a few dates, but we always go to the movies or a chain Italian restaurant. This feels different. Nice, but definitely different.

"Where are we going?" I ask as we walk.

The air is warm, but the breeze that drifts past us is just cool enough to keep you from getting hot.

"Shopping."

"A girl could always go shopping," I say with a laugh.

"I need to pick out something for my mom. Maybe you can help."

Sadness clutches at me for my own mom, but pride that he wants my help overshadows that. We find a small trinket shop and step inside. It smells like oranges in the quaint shop. He makes a beeline over to an array of dog-themed glass collectibles.

"She likes dogs?" I ask, picking up a Doberman figurine.

"Not that kind," he says with a chuckle before pointing at one of the glass Yorkies.

"Aww," I say with a smile. "It's cute. You should get it for her."

"My mom makes a great meatloaf. You should come Sunday to dinner with me."

I dart my gaze to his. He's no longer looking at the decorations, but searing his green eyes into me.

"You want me to meet your mom?"

He cups my cheek. "More importantly, I want my mom to meet you." He chuckles. "I can't promise she won't drive you crazy, though. You'll be the first woman I've ever brought home for her to meet."

This has me gaping. "The first one? Ever?"

He shrugs like it's no big deal. But it's huge. It blows my mind he's never been in such a relationship with a woman that he'd introduce her to his mother, yet here I am, barely blown into his life and he's asking for that very thing.

"I'll go with you." I pause, furrowing my brows. "I think Mom would have wanted me to get out of the house and not mope around."

His lips quirk up on one side. "It's a date then. Another one."

"As long as you keep your promise about what happens *after* date one, then I'll so be looking forward to date two."

He dips down and kisses the top of my head while copping a feel of my ass. "Oh, that's a promise."

We manage to pay and leave the shop without jumping each other's bones. I tuck the trinket away in my purse and we continue on our trek. When we come to an old, used bookstore, I let out a little squeal of delight. Daniel laughs and opens the door to the shop for me.

As soon as I walk in, I inhale the musty but familiar scent of books. I wasn't a reader until Mom got sick. Sitting by someone's bedside while they slept tends to get boring. Social media doesn't offer the same escape that a book does. And when I was aching so badly, an escape was exactly what I needed.

This particular bookstore is one I haven't been in, and the thrill of an exciting new adventure looms. I walk straight over to the classics, hunting for the oldest looking versions of my favorites I can find. I love photographing them for my blog. From the corner of my eye, I take note of Daniel browsing a section nearby. My heart flutters that he's left me to my own devices. A girl could get lost for hours in a bookstore.

An hour comes and goes quickly. I've piled up five of my favorites including a ratty copy of *Wuthering Heights*. My stomach grumbles, signifying it's time to eat soon.

"She emerges from the book haze," Daniel teases when I round a corner on my hunt for him.

He's kicked back in a lounge chair with his feet up on the coffee table looking like he owns the place. If he did, then I'd crawl into his lap and have a repeat of last night to thank him for taking me here. Since we're not alone, I dip down and press a kiss to his cheek.

"Thank you, Dr. Dan."

"For what?"

I sigh and smile. "For being you."

He rises from his seat, grips my hips, and hauls me against him. My handful of books are smashed between us. I tilt my head up to admire his handsome face.

"Thank you for being you too," he murmurs before giving me a kiss that most likely makes everyone in the bookstore blush.

CHAPTER
nine

Daniel

T he look on her face in the bookstore was one of pure bliss. Happiness on Lauren's face looks really good. It makes me want to do everything humanly possible to keep it there.

"Sorry I took so long," she says absently, leaning her head against my shoulder as we walk.

"I thought you were enjoying yourself."

"I was. But I know that might have been boring for you."

I chuckle. "Are you kidding me? Watching you turn absolutely giddy with excitement over those books was my own form of entertainment."

"Good, because I haven't had that much fun in a long time."

She turns quiet as we walk and I hate how sad she sounded. An eighteen-year-old girl who's just graduated from high school should have the world at her fingertips. It's as though she's been caged and I freed her for the day.

"What are your plans now that you've graduated?"

"I haven't allowed myself to think about it," she admits.

I stop and turn to face her. The warm wind sends her golden blond hair fluttering behind her. With the lowering sun shining on her, she's every bit the angel I nicknamed her. I almost expect her to sprout wings and fly off to the heavens. Instead, she stays grounded, frowning at me. Lost. Sad. Confused. Distant.

Gently gripping her chin, I tilt her head up and steal a chaste kiss. "You should be thinking about what you want. You have your whole life in front of you."

Her brown eyes grow misty and she darts them away. "Do I?" The bitterness in her words startles me. In half a second, I go from doting boyfriend to concerned doctor. I assess her pretty face and note her skin is pale despite the blush she's applied. The circles under her eyes are barely hidden beneath a layer of makeup. Her shoulders are slightly sagging. She's tired and worn down—from the inside out. But why?

"Should we leave?" I ask, suddenly feeling like a tool for walking her all through downtown and wearing her out.

"W-What? No. Why would we leave?" she demands, the fire back in her voice as she glares at me.

I rub my thumb over her bottom lip. "Then where'd you go just then?"

It wasn't here. It was some dark place in her

mind and it slipped out for me to see. My heart hasn't stopped hammering in my chest since she uttered those bitter words.

"Nowhere," she says with a one-shouldered shrug. "I'm hungry. Are we almost there?"

I want to demand answers, but I also don't want to ruin our date. It takes everything in me to keep my promise and not nag her. At least not now. I don't want to damper the moment. But we will have this conversation. Soon.

"Another block. Need a piggy-back ride?" I say with a wide grin.

She laughs. "I mean, if you're offering…"

A challenge.

I squat and pat my shoulder. "Hop on, little girl."

"Little girl?" she huffs but hands me her purse that's stuffed with her bag of books.

Smirking, I take it as she grabs my shoulders and then hooks her legs around my waist. Once she's latched on, I hold her heavy purse for her with one arm and the back of her thigh with the other. It makes me feel better to carry her knowing she's tired.

But as soon as we start walking, we get the looks.

Some are amused. Some are questioning. And some are downright disgusted.

"That woman was glaring at us," Lauren says, her chin resting on my shoulder. "Think maybe I flashed her by accident."

"Nah, she was just being a bitch."

I walk us down the block and before we get there, Lauren squirms to be let down. Finally, I relent and set her to her feet.

"We're not there yet," I tell her, frowning.

She scowls at someone passing by until they look away. "I'll walk."

I take her hand and give it a squeeze. We've barely made it fifty steps before she blows up.

"Do you have a problem?" she demands of a couple walking by.

The snooty woman huffs. "You don't have to flaunt it."

"Flaunt what?" I growl.

Her husband has the sense to start pulling the woman away.

"That," the woman says, waving a manicured hand at us. "The sugar daddy nonsense."

Anger boils in my gut, but it's Lauren who blows a gasket first.

"How in the hell is this any of your business, lady?" Lauren bellows. "I swear to God people like you are what's wrong with the world today. Maybe you should be more concerned over the fact your husband's eyes haven't left my cleavage the whole time we've been here!"

The woman gapes at her and then smacks her husband. I take my cue to grab the girl and go. Lauren curses as I all but drag her toward the restaurant away from the couple. Once we're outside the restaurant, I stop and place my hands on her shoulders.

"Calm down," I state, leaning my forehead against hers.

"Calm down? These assholes need to get a fucking life." Her face is red and her chest heaves with her furious rant.

I caress her cheek and kiss her softly, hoping to quell the rage. It works because she relaxes and gives in to the kiss.

"You ready to eat?" I ask, my lips grazing hers.

"Yeah," she grumbles. "I didn't mean to explode. They just kept staring at us like we're some kind of freak show. You don't look that old and I'm freaking eighteen. It's stupid. I wanted to slap the looks off every single face that walked by."

"I should have warned you," I say, pulling away.

"That everyone's an asshole?"

"Well, that too." I chuckle and tuck a golden strand of hair behind her ear. "Morris warned me that being with a much younger woman would come at a price." I motion from the way we came. "Stares. Disgust."

"Fuck them," she growls.

"I agree, angel. I'm sorry they're looking at us like we're doing something wrong."

"We're not doing anything wrong." The haughtiness in her tone makes me smile.

"Nothing wrong at all." I wink at her. "All the wrong stuff we'll save for later when I have you in my bed."

∾

"It's breathtaking up here," Lauren says, the grin never leaving her face.

Morris did me a solid by suggesting this place. The rooftop dining has a charming but trendy feel to it. The view is amazing and our timing is perfect with the sun beginning to set. But it's the view right in front of me that steals the show.

Fuck, she's so gorgeous.

There's an innocence to her that has the inner beast inside me craving to defile and mark and own. But that innocence also begs me to protect and nurture. The innocence gets long forgotten each time her sweet laugh dances through the air or the way her pink lips pout when she's unhappy about something. I'm fixated on the pale column of her throat that would look good painted red from my mouth and scruff. The valley between her breasts, though, is what calls to my dick. A light sheen of sweat glistens there and I'd give up my car just to run my tongue there, lapping at her salty sweetness.

"I'm not on the menu," she teases, her brown eyes alight with mischief as she watches me.

"Not yet. Later."

I'm still admiring her when a man approaches our table. Much younger. He seems familiar, though I can't place him.

"Dr. Venable?" he asks, sticking out his hand for me to shake.

I return the gesture to shake his hand. "That I am. I feel like I know you."

"Aiden," he says with a wide grin. "I broke my wrist a while back. You were the ER doctor on duty."

"Ahhh, Aiden with the broody twin? Right?"

He laughs. "That's us. So cool to have you here. Although, I was warned. Vaughn told me you'd be here for dinner and to save the best seat for you."

"You work here?" I ask.

"Own it along with my partners." He gives me a devilish wink that I'm unsure how to interpret. "What can I get you two lovebirds?"

"A bottle of your house wine will be great to start," I say with a smile. "And your best appetizer."

"I'm afraid I'll need to see some ID." His features grow stern. Then, he starts to laugh. "Man, I couldn't even say that with a straight face. You guys are cool. Don't tell anyone you're getting special treatment."

He saunters off and I meet Lauren's amused stare.

"Fancy doctor gets spoiled around here," she teases.

"Yeah, yeah," I grunt out.

"So what made you decide to be a doctor?" She sips on her water as she stares off in the sunset. I could stare at her delicate, feminine profile forever.

"Oh God," I groan. "It's kind of embarrassing."

"Now I really need to know."

"I was in college, living my best life, when my roommate Dale got me hooked on this new show called *ER*. I didn't even want to watch the show, but he lured me in by name dropping Michael Crichton as the creator of the show. Since I was already a fan of his work, I sat down with Dale and quickly got hooked on it." I rub at my neck and chuckle. "All the guys our age were living the typical bachelor college life, but not Dale and me. We both brainstormed on changing our majors from business to medicine."

"He sounds like a good friend," she says, her brown eyes twinkling.

"He was."

Aiden brings the bottle of wine, two glasses, and some cheese fries with bacon all over them. He gives me a nod and thankfully leaves to let me chat with my date.

"Was?"

"Yeah," I reply with a sigh. "Cancer took him about ten years ago."

"I'm so sorry."

"I hated how ironic it was for the doctor to die from an illness he couldn't treat. I still have lunch with his wife and son from time to time to catch up. He'd want me to check in on them, you know?"

"That's awfully sweet of you. And here I didn't think the good doctor could get any better?"

"Oh," I tease with a smirk. "It gets much better."

She laughs as she pulls some cheese fries onto a plate. We both get engrossed in talking about how delicious the food is. Aiden stops by to ask for our order before making himself absent again. The sky goes through its daily change from bright blue, to orange and pink and purple, to dark navy as evening falls. I'm thankful the view was so breathtaking and we got to admire the sunset.

The steak is great, but the company is even better. When we finally finish, Aiden brings out a molten chocolate lava cake that's "on the house." Hearing Lauren moan in such an enticing way makes me want to throw all the money in my wallet at Aiden.

"Want a bite?" she asks, licking her plump lips.

"Yes."

Based on the wicked gleam in her eyes, I think she knows we're both talking about something other than the dessert. When she holds out a fork, I take the bait and sample the cake. Rich and sweet and gooey.

"Good, huh?"

"Absolutely." I sit back and sip my wine. "Now what? Do you want to go somewhere after this?"

"Your house," she murmurs.

As much as my dick convinces us that it's because she wants to fuck, I can see the fatigue wearing on her. It worries the hell out of me.

"Sure thing, angel. Let me get the check."

She smiles and puts on a brave face for me, but

something is wrong. And if I didn't think she'd run, I'd take her to the ER right now. Have them do every test imaginable so we can find out what lurks within her and fix it.

But she'd hate me.

And I can't have that when I haven't even given her a chance to love me.

CHAPTER
ten

Lauren

Holy shit.

I expected his house to be nice, being a doctor and all, but I didn't expect it to be this nice. When we arrived twenty minutes ago, he gave me the grand tour. We bypassed where Jenna stays and I'm glad. It feels a little awkward to meet my new boyfriend's daughter who's my age only to disappear with him to his bedroom. No one wants to imagine their dad fucking, no matter how hot he is to everyone else. I'd feel grossed out if someone was to do that with my dad.

So, when we snuck off to his bedroom and he shut us safely inside, I was finally able to breathe easier.

But now that we're alone, I can feel my nerves fraying. Last night was so easy. We'd practically fucked on my bed. Until this moment, I'd been ready to go.

"You okay?" Daniel asks, his green eyes assessing me.

"Yep," I squeak out, forcing a smile.

He walks over to me and cups my cheek. "You know if you don't want to do anything, we don't have to. I'm perfectly happy with going into the living room and watching a movie with you. As long as I get to hold your hand and kiss you, I'm happy."

I melt a little at his words. "I'm just nervous."

"You don't have to be with me," he assures me. "You set the pace. I'm just here for the ride." He winks at me, setting my insides on fire.

"Maybe we could take a bath." I bite on my bottom lip, frowning at him. "Is that okay?"

He laughs. "Relax, angel. If you want to bathe with me, that's what we'll do. I wanted to make this date perfect and your opinion weighs heavily on that."

God, why does he have to be so damn wonderful?

"A bath," I tell him. "And bubbles if you have any." I tap my chin in thought. "Candles?"

"Anything else, your highness?" He smirks at me.

"Yeah, smartass, maybe you can fan me and feed me grapes too."

His green eyes twinkle with amusement before he disappears into his large bathroom. I kick off my cowgirl boots and peel off my socks. The water begins running and a few minutes later, he exits the bathroom as I'm tying my hair up in a bun.

"Need help?" he asks, gesturing at my dress.

I could manage the zipper myself, but a thrill shoots through me with the thought of him doing it for me. Turning away from him, I offer my back to him.

His heat scorches me as he steps close. When his lips press against the back of my neck, I smile.

"You're beautiful, Lauren. I can honestly say, I've never seen anyone more fucking pretty than you."

"You're pretty hot yourself, Dr. Dan."

He chuckles as he grips the zipper and eases it down its path. The cool air kisses my flesh as it's exposed. His palms caress my bare back and then he pushes the fabric over my shoulders. The dress hits the floor with a soft sound, pooling at my feet. He expertly unhooks my strapless bra, allowing that too to fall to the floor. My nipples harden in anticipation.

"A thong looks good on you," he rumbles, his hands gripping each ass cheek and squeezing. "A perfect ass should always be on display." His thumbs hook into the top of my panties and he slides them off me. They drop to the floor with the rest of my clothes.

"Seems unfair I'm naked and you're not," I say with a breathless pout.

"I'll rectify that soon, angel. Besides, I still have some unmet demands to fulfil." He swats my ass, leaving a stinging handprint on my skin. "Get in the bath and wait for me."

"Bossy," I grumble.

"You like it." He swats me again, sending me on my way.

It's true. I do like it. I like him. Us together. The feeling of normalcy and hope threaded together. I hadn't realized just how hopeless I'd been since Mom died that it seems so unique and beautiful staring me in the face.

His bathroom is fit for a king. Giant. Fancy as hell. The scent of lavender fills my nostrils and he already has several candles burning on the tub ledge. Bubbles are growing as the water fills. I haven't taken a bath in ages. Never with a man. I'm eager and nervous all at once.

The water is nice and warm but not too hot. When I sit down, the bath is already filled enough for two people, so I turn off the water. It's quiet as I wait for him. My side throbs with pain and I wince. It started up at dinner, but I sure as hell wasn't about to admit that to Daniel. I don't know if I hurt myself with all the walking or what.

I lean back and close my eyes, breathing slowly in hopes that the pain passes. Footsteps pad into the bathroom and I peek out from beneath my lashes.

God, he's so gorgeous.

He's missing his shirt and I'm shocked to find tattoos on one side of his ribs. It looks like black stitches and staples holding his side together. Words are written in cursive on his side. I'm curious until my eyes slide to the prominent V-shaped muscles that are his lower abdomen. I feel embarrassed of my small pooch of a stomach—that I blame on lack of exercise from not feeling well all the time—because he seems as though he's etched in stone.

"You need me to hold still so you can get your fill?" he asks, an amused grin tugging at his lips.

With a body like his, a playful smile, and a full head of dark hair, he doesn't look a day over twenty-five. Damn, he looks good.

"I'm waiting for the grand finale," I tease, dipping my stare to his boxers.

Beneath the fabric, his cock is thick inside. And he's not even hard. Just boxers filled with a gigantic penis that I've had the pleasure of rubbing on.

"I wouldn't be a gracious host if I left you waiting," he says with a teasing lilt in his voice. He sets down a bowl of grapes and a bottle of wine beside the tub before disappearing. A few minutes later he returns with some glasses. He fills the wineglasses up and then, with his eyes on me, he pulls off his boxers.

Now he's hard.

His cock is impressive to look at. Long. Thick. Veiny. I'd seen it for just a bit last night, but in the bright lights of the bathroom, I am able to inspect every fine detail.

"Don't forget the lights," I remind him.

As much as I want to look at him, I'd rather not compare bodies. Mine needs work and his is too perfect for words. His brow lifts in that way that makes me think he's watching my every move and focusing on every detail. He hits the lights and returns to the tub. The water rises with his weight as he sinks in with me. His arm hooks around my waist and he pulls me between his legs with my back resting against his chest.

I'm wound tight with nerves, but the moment he hands me my wine, I relax. I don't know what I was expecting. Maybe for him to launch into fucking me or turn filthy. It would have been fine but...

I need this more.

Comfort.

His nurturing nature.

Gentle caresses and the way he inhales my hair when he doesn't think I notice.

It's been so long since I've been held and cared for.

When a grape probes at my lips, I laugh before accepting it. "You know we just ate, right?"

"You looked hungry," he says with a chuckle.

"For cock," I tease.

His palm splays over my stomach. "I'll feed you that later."

With his hand on my swollen stomach, I fidget. When I fidget, it makes the pain worsen. I breathe through my nose, fighting tears.

"Everything okay?"

"Perfect," I breathe, forcing my emotion out

of my date and back into the dark corner where it belongs.

"What does your tattoo mean?" I ask, gently pushing his hand away from my stomach.

He stiffens from behind me before gulping down his wine. His hand settles on my thigh this time. I give it a squeeze. Much better there.

"I didn't realize how hard I was searching for happiness. Like I knew there was something I wanted out of life, I just didn't know what exactly. It was like part of my soul was gone and I needed to find it." He rubs my thigh in a gentle way. "When I got into medical school, I felt it. The pull toward medicine. It was like my body and mind woke up, but we were still missing something. When I helped my first real patient—brought them back from the brink of death—I knew. I was put on this earth to heal people. It completed a part of me. My tattoo represents the finding of my soul out there and pulling it back into my body that's stitched back together, holding it in."

"You're a good doctor," I whisper.

I wonder if he had known my mom, would it have made any difference.

"Lauren," he says softly, his mouth against my ear. "Talk to me. Something's wrong."

"I'm scared," I choke out. Not of him or our date or our bath. "Of the unknown."

"Sometimes not knowing is worse," he utters.

"Knowledge gives you some semblance of power. The unknown can be something you can eradicate."

"But what happens when the unknown becomes a horrific reality? Then what?"

He inhales my hair before kissing my head. "Then you lean on the ones who care about you. You face that reality with others, never alone, angel."

I turn my head to find his mouth. Our kiss tastes like wine and understanding. His tongue is firm and powerful, but he holds on to me like he can protect me from anything. I want so badly for that to be true. I know if it were in his power, he'd protect me from whatever threw itself at me.

"I want you to make love to me, Daniel," I murmur, brushing my lips on his. "And then…"

"And then what?"

"And then I need you to take care of me."

Before the words have left my lips, he scoops me in his arms, lifting me from the tub. Water splashes everywhere as he steps out and sets me to my feet. He's intense and thorough as he dries off every part of me. Once he's sure I'm dry, he wraps me in a dry towel before quickly drying himself off. His towel falls to the floor and then this god of a naked man scoops me up again. He's gentle and caring as he totes me into his bedroom.

"If anything hurts, tell me," he says as he sets me on the bed. The covers have been drawn down and the sheets are soft.

"I will," I vow.

He presses a kiss to my lips before turning off the lights. The glow from the candles in the bathroom gives the bedroom a dark, but romantic feel. I toss away the towel as he prowls into bed with me. At first, his body warms mine from beside me as he kisses me unrushed. Heat rushes just beneath the surface of my skin, the ache to be touched overwhelming me. He must sense my need because he touches my breasts, one at a time, tweaking each nipple.

"Your tits are so fucking addictive," he rumbles, nipping at my bottom lip. "I love feeling them in my hands."

My heart rate quickens and I squirm with need. "I like you touching them."

His hand slides over my distended stomach, lingering for a long moment. "Are you sure you're okay to do this?" he asks, his voice tight with worry.

"I need you to make love to me, Daniel. I need one night of normalcy."

He nods before kissing down my neck to my nipple. I whimper when he bites on it and pulls. His mouth slides over a large part of my breast and he sucks on damn near the whole thing. Hard.

I cry out in a mix of pleasure and pain. At least he's not holding back. I'd probably die if he treated me like I was fragile. I don't want to be dealt with as though I'm a wilting flower. I want to be ripped apart, throttled, used, and abused. Sexually, of course. And then I want his perfect mouth to put me back together again. I want him to heal me in a way only he can—a way that has nothing to do with his training.

He grips my thigh, parting me open, and then his fingers are at my pussy. With expert urgency, he massages my clit. Zings of pleasure pulsate through me, matching the cadence of the pounding in my head. I wanted one pain-free night and to make love to the man I've grown to care deeply for, but clearly that's not going to happen. I grit my teeth and ignore the usual hurts to focus on the new pleasures. Each time he brings me close to climax, he pulls away from my clit to tease my opening that grows wetter by the second.

"I'm going to taste you now," he rumbles, kissing my lower stomach with a soft brush of his lips. "Do you want my mouth on your pussy, angel?"

I let out a harsh breath. "I do."

He chuckles, sending vibrations of need coursing through me. "I do too. I bet you taste like heaven."

I smirk at his corniness. "Might taste a little like fire too."

His tongue circles my clit but doesn't touch it. He simply teases my pussy lips with his wet tongue. I can't help but lift my hips, seeking his hot mouth.

"Greedy girl," he chides, pressing a kiss to my clit and making me gasp. "You're not patient at all."

"Nope," I sass. "I want you to make me come with your tongue."

"Just my tongue?" he growls as he slides a finger

into my warmth. "Or can I use this too?" He curls his finger into me, rubbing against something magical within me.

"Holy shit," I curse.

"She swears like a naughty angel."

I laugh. "I'm going to swear a lot more if you keep teasing me."

Rather than mouthing off, he literally uses his mouth. I cry out in shock when he sucks hard on my clit. It's dizzying and sends fire burning through my every nerve ending. My head throbs, but I don't even care anymore because it feels too good. His wicked finger strums me from within, making me see stars.

Holy hell, this feels good.

My body trembles and tenses, drawing nearer to ecstasy with each passing second. The room spins and my skin flushes. His tongue laps at my clit in a teasing way and then he's circling it with purpose.

"Oh God," I whimper, my back arching up.

He chooses that moment to suck on my clit again at the exact time he applies pressure to the spot inside me that feels so good.

Then. I. Freaking. Explode.

His tongue slows down as does his finger as he gently unwinds me from the most intense orgasm I've ever had. He pulls away and flashes me a wicked grin that lights up the darkness.

"Spread your legs, angel, I'm about to make you mine."

CHAPTER
eleven

Daniel

My body buzzes with pent-up energy as I fetch a condom from the drawer and roll it on my dick that aches to be inside my girl. Yeah, my fucking girl. Watching her lose her mind with her orgasm was one of the best things I've ever experienced. I can't wait to feel her body writhing beneath mine the next time it happens.

As I climb on the bed and prowl over her, I watch for signs of distress. She's hurting, that much is clear. I wanted to yank her out of that tub and take her to the hospital, but she's super goddamn stubborn. She wants to make love without anything hanging over her head. Truth is, I want that for her.

Because come tomorrow…

I can't think about it.

I have a bad fucking feeling, but I won't let it ruin tonight. I swore I'd turn off doctor mode for one night and show her the best night of her life. We'll deal with tomorrow…tomorrow.

Tonight is ours.

"You're beautiful," I praise as I settle between spread thighs. My dick rubs against her slick cunt. I'd love to feel her bare, but we haven't discussed birth control, and the last thing Lauren needs in her life is fear of pregnancy.

"So are you," she says breathily. "I want to kiss you."

"You want to taste your sweet honey on my tongue?" I tease.

She giggles and fuck if it isn't the lightest sound in the world. "You're a filthy doctor."

"And you're a filthy girl. Look at us…a perfect pair."

Her fingers thread into my hair and she pulls me to her. Our mouths meet gently at first but when my tongue swipes across hers, she lets out a groan. She rakes her fingernails through my scalp, kissing me urgently.

"I'm big and you're small," I warn. "It's going to be a stretch. All it takes is one word. I'll stop, angel. Understood?"

She nods. "I'm ready. I can handle pain."

It makes my heart skip a beat for her. I hate that she even knows the meaning of pain. I want to take it all away. At the very least, I can give her body some well-deserved love. I kiss her deeply as I grab hold of my cock. Running the tip through her juices, I tease her opening, warning her of what's to come. Her heels dig into my ass, urging me forward.

I'm so close.

The tip of my cock slides between her lips, pressing against her tight entrance, demanding a way in. Her body is hot as it slowly grips mine around the fat mushroomed head of my dick. She sucks in a sharp breath.

"Keep going," she breathes.

I inch forward, slowly, for two reasons. One, so I don't rip her apart by accident. And two, so I don't blow my load in a half a second.

"That's it," I croon. "Relax and take me, angel. I'll fit. Every thick inch will fit, but you have to let me in."

She moans, spreading wider. Her body grips me to the point I nearly black out from pleasure. Gently, I pull out some to coat my cock with her juices and then slide in some more. Little by little, inch by inch. I fuck her with shallow thrusts until I feel that her body has fully accepted me. Then, I drive into her deep, flexing my ass as I plunge into her tight depths.

"Oh God!" she cries out, her fingernails ripping at my hair.

"You okay?" I murmur, pressing kisses to her mouth. "I can stop."

"N-No. Don't stop."

"I'm in, Lauren. All the way in. How does it feel?"

"Crazy," she says with a breathy giggle. "It hurts too, but the good kind of hurt. I can't believe you're inside me."

"Believe it." I kiss her mouth and then nip along

her jaw to her neck. Sucking on her flesh, I love the way her cunt clenches around me. My breath is hot against her skin as I say, "Now I'm going to make love to you."

With slow, measured thrusts, I drive into my sweet girl, owning her body. She slides her fingernails to my shoulders, clawing me there. I love that she's marking me and leaving her own bites of pain on me. I suck on her neck hard and then bite her, picking up my pace. Our bodies quickly grow slick with sweat and our need to touch and feel every part of the other person becomes frantic and obsessive.

More. More. More.

I just want more of her.

My slow lovemaking turns wild as I buck into her. Fucking. With the intense way she scratches her nails over my biceps and the way she moans like a feral cat, there's no denying we've graduated past virginal lovemaking. She's mine and I'm claiming her. She wants to be claimed.

More. More. More.

"Oh God, Daniel!"

Her body begins shaking like it did when I owned her with my tongue. I drive into her hard, grinding my hips in such a way, I punish her clit some with the movement. It does the trick because she screams out my name a second before she detonates.

Fuck.

Her body squeezes around my dick over and over like it's fisting me to climax. I can't hold on any longer, giving in to the satisfaction of my orgasm. My nuts draw up in pleasure and I release an animalistic growl as I grind against her. Cum fills the condom and because of how long I've gone without getting laid, I'm worried it's going to fucking explode inside her.

"Jesus, Lauren," I groan. "You trying to give this old man a heart attack?"

She laughs and grips my hair so I'm forced to look at her. "Don't die on me, Gramps. I'd like to try that again a time or two."

Lifting a brow, I smirk at her. "Just one or two? I'm old, but not that damn old."

"So we'll get to do that at least three times?"

"At least three tonight alone," I tease.

I pull out of her to go dispose of the condom. My heart is racing in my chest. Once it's gone, I come back over to her to and pull her out of bed.

"Bath is probably still warm." I hug her naked body to mine. "Want to wash off before bed?"

She sags against me, weak and tired. "Yeah."

We both know the one time was all she had in her tonight, but it's fun to tease. Truth is, I don't know if she'll even make it to the bathroom. I scoop her in my arms and carry her back to the tub.

"Daniel?" she says as we sink down into the still-warm water.

"Yeah, angel?"

"That was amazing. Thank you."

She grows quiet and then a sob escapes her. I tense up, hugging her to me.

"What is it, baby?" I whisper, my chest aching.

"Can we go to the hospital now?"

Fuck.

We don't have tomorrow.

We only have tonight.

❧

I pace around outside the radiology department as Lauren gets her MRI. I'm going to be sick. When Morris's face paled as he looked at the ultrasound, I knew something was wrong. He immediately ordered an MRI to get a closer look. At her kidneys.

"Still in there?" he asks as he comes striding down the hall, a rare, serious expression on his face.

I nod and swallow. "The ultrasound looked bad."

So many dark masses I'd seen on the screen. So fucking many.

"The MRI will tell us the size and number of kidney cysts she has," he tells me like I'm not a fucking doctor too. "Then, we can evaluate the amount of healthy kidney tissue she has."

"She needs a specialist to be sure," I state bitterly. I know I'm insulting my friend, but thankfully he softens, understanding I'm just stressed as hell.

"Of course," he placates. "A specialist will confirm, but we both know what we're looking at, Daniel."

Autosomal dominant polycystic kidney disease.

"It usually doesn't manifest until a person's thirties or forties," I argue.

"Usually," he says. "Her mom had kidney disease too?"

"I don't have her history, just what Lauren's told me. Something similar if not the same thing." I close my eyes and pinch the bridge of my nose. "Her mom died."

He grips my shoulder. "Listen, man. Whatever it is, she'll get the best care. We'll make sure of it."

I lift my gaze to his, hating that emotion burns in my eyes. "I don't want to lose her. I just fucking found her."

He pulls me in for a hug. "Don't go zero to a hundred. She's going to hate it if you're already planning her funeral. So drop that shit right here because she's going to need your medical brain and strength. Together, you two can get through this."

"When did you become so wise?" I grumble.

"I had a good role model." He pats me on the back. "You can do this. So can she."

I sure fucking hope so.

He runs off to deal with another patient. When the door clicks open, Lauren steps through it, looking as pale as the gown she's wearing. I swoop in and wrap an arm around her waist.

"How did it go?"

"It was fine," she says tightly.

"Let's get you back to your room."

Once she's settled in her bed, I crawl into the bed beside her. She curls up against me. Her body feels cold and she shivers. I pull the covers over her, warming her up.

"I'm scared," she murmurs. "I should call my brother or my dad, but I don't want to yet. Not until I know what I'm dealing with."

I stroke my fingers through her hair. "We won't know until the radiologist offers his expert opinion, but I can offer what I saw and determined myself."

"What do you think?"

"Autosomal dominant polycystic kidney disease. Those dark masses on the ultrasound looked like that way at least. When there are twenty or more present—"

"Twenty or more?" she says, her tone shrill. "I don't want them. How do we make them go away?"

My heart breaks for her. "Let's wait until he comes in. He'll explain it better."

She grips my jaw, tugging my face to meet hers. "I don't want his explanation. I want yours."

"If any cysts are bleeding, ruptured, or infected, they'll need to be treated accordingly. Depending on the severity of them, you may need further treatment."

"I got this from my mom," she says sadly. "Right? I could give this to my kids one day?"

I stroke her hair from her face and kiss her forehead. "ADPKD is either acquired or hereditary. Considering what happened with your mother, it's probably safe to assume it's hereditary."

The door opens and Phil walks in. His brows are furled. When he sees me curled around Lauren, he gives me a sympathetic smile. He sits down and pulls the chair close.

"How are you doing?" he asks her.

She lets out a harsh sigh. "Dr. Dan here was just giving me a preview of what you're going to tell me. Am I going to die like Mom?"

He flinches slightly at her blunt delivery. "Let's not get ahead of ourselves here, Lauren. I'll be frank with you because you clearly need me to be. It doesn't look good. I'm shocked at the quantity of cysts on your kidneys, especially your right one. I believe the ones on the left can be treated with diet regulation of salt and protein intake. With proper medications, we can control your hypertension and renal stones. If that right kidney starts giving us problems, then we may progress to dialysis and transplantation at a later stage."

"So I'm not dying?"

"Your body is sick right now, but it's still in a controllable state. If you stick to what your specialist requires, you'll live a higher quality of life than if you let it slip. You cannot afford to let it slip."

As he continues to discuss her options and treatment, I squeeze her hand and hope to hell I can help her through this.

I need her to be okay.

CHAPTER
twelve

Lauren

One week later...

My phone buzzes, but I can't look at it. I'm tired and I feel empty inside. It's like this when Daniel goes to work. I have nothing or no one to occupy my time. My thoughts consume me.

Dad has been home for two days, but I can't bring myself to tell him what's wrong with me. He's off having dinner with Landon. I want to tell him, but I can't break his heart again. He was so broken when Mom died.

My tears soak my pillow as I cry silently. I notice several texts from Daniel, but I don't have the energy to respond. I already feel horrible for missing dinner with his mom because of my issues. When I hear the garage door opening, I drag myself out of bed and pad downstairs. Landon and Dad are playfully swatting at each other in the middle of the kitchen. They look similar—both tall and handsome. Smiling.

I should go.

Not kill the mood.

But it's too late.

"Hey, sleepyhead," Landon says, thrusting a bag my way. "We brought you a burger and fries from Sandy's. Your favorites." He waggles his brows at me.

While Landon is amused, Dad's smile has fallen as he inspects me with intense scrutiny.

"I'm actually going to heat up some chicken and vegetables," I mutter. Last night, Daniel cooked me a healthy meal that fits within my new dietary restrictions. I brought leftovers home with me.

"Are you sick?" Landon jokes. "Since when do you turn down Sandy's?"

I flinch at the word sick. Dad's gaze narrows.

"Honey, come here," Dad orders, holding his arms open.

It's then, I break.

At first it was a crack and then I just shatter. Right at his feet. On the kitchen floor with my brother watching in horror. I collapse to the floor, my emotion consuming me like a savage tidal wave of grief. I'm drowning in it.

Strong warm arms envelope me. I'm pulled into my dad's embrace as my brother takes my hand. I'm choking on my tears, the words unable to find their way out.

"Talk to me, baby girl," Dad pleads. "Tell me what's wrong."

"Yeah, who do we need to beat up?" Landon growls.

I tremble in their arms. "I'm s-so sorry, Daddy," I sob. "I'm s-sorry."

"Shhh," Dad says, stroking my hair. "Tell me what's wrong so I can fix it."

But he can't fix this.

"Autosomal dominant polycystic kidney disease," I blurt out.

He tenses, but then kisses my head. "How do you know this?"

I cling to him, crying. "I went to the ER and c-confirmed my s-suspicions. I still need to see a specialist, but my kidneys are a mess."

Dad scoops me up and carries me into the living room. We sit on the couch and Landon drops on my other side. When I look at my brother, I see that he's crying too. And that makes me cry harder.

Landon squeezes my hand. "Is this why you've been sick for months and months?"

"I don't want to die," I tell them, quaking with emotion.

Dad's body shakes as he cries, but he quickly composes himself. His voice is gruff and firm. "I won't let that happen."

"But Mom," I argue.

"Your mother went years and years ignoring her body until it was too late." He kisses my hair. "And while you tried to keep it from us, because you're just like her, it's out now. We can work toward keeping you healthy. No more secrets, baby girl. From here on out, I want to be apprised of everything. I'll go to all your appointments."

"I guess it helps I'm dating a doctor too," I blurt out.

Dad stiffens, pulling away. His eyes are bloodshot from crying and his cheeks are wet, but anger flickers in his dark blues. "A doctor?"

"The hot ER doctor Winter is always rambling about?" Landon offers.

I sometimes forget his girlfriend is best friends with Winter, who basically introduced me to Daniel when she brought me into the ER that day.

"Yeah, Dr. Venable. His name is Daniel."

"Daniel Venable?" Dad hisses. "I know him."

"You do?"

"Well, I know of him. We have mutual friends. Lauren, he's my age," Dad growls. "What the hell?"

My spine straightens and I pin Dad with a firm glare. "Don't start. Not now. He's kind and caring. Not some monster trying to seduce away your little girl. I'm eighteen and can make my own decisions about who I date."

He opens his mouth to speak when someone knocks on the front door.

Oh crap.

Daniel had been texting me and I blew it off, which means...

He's here.

"I'll get it," Landon says, hopping up and running off.

A moment later, Daniel strides in still wearing scrubs and a tired expression. When he sees me, he rushes over to us, dropping into the spot Landon vacated beside me.

"I've been texting and calling you. I was worried sick," Daniel chides, grabbing both my hands in his. "How are you feeling?"

Dad practically thrums with fury beside me.

"Fine," I lie. "Uh, Daniel, meet my dad, Teddy. Dad, this is my boyfriend."

Daniel's eyes scrutinize me for a second before he darts his attention to my dad.

"Mr. Englewood," Daniel says, his voice polite but strained with worry. "It's nice to meet you." He offers his hand and Dad reluctantly shakes it.

"You do realize Lauren is eighteen," Dad bites out, blunt as hell. "And you're what? Forty?"

"Forty-five."

Landon crosses his arms over his chest and scowls at us, looking just like freaking Dad. I stick my tongue out at him. He smirks and relaxes.

"Don't you think you're too old for her?" Dad demands.

Daniel squeezes my hand. "I understand what it looks like to an outsider, I'll give you that. But Lauren and I have an intense connection. I'm not stringing her along or forcing her to do anything. I want nothing but her happiness and to take care of her."

"I can take care of her," Dad growls. "I can make my daughter happy."

"Dad—"

"No, Lauren, I'm not going to have some old ass man swoop in and confuse my daughter—"

"Where were you this entire year?" Daniel demands, his voice icy cold.

"I beg your pardon," Dad says.

"Working. While you were off working and her brother was with his girlfriend, Lauren was all alone. She was dealing with something no one needs to deal with on their own." He darts his eyes my way, questions dancing in them.

"They know," I assure him.

Even in the heat of the moment, he respects my secrets.

"I'm not insulting you, Teddy," Daniel says, "I'm just speaking the truth. We met through the hospital and kept meeting. I took care of her because she was all alone. Then, it just evolved. I'm not sure when it happened, but it did. I'd do anything to keep her healthy and happy."

"Lauren," Dad says, pain in his voice. "I didn't know. Had I known, I would've already come back to work in town. I can tell the office I can no longer travel. Things will change. I will be here for you, baby girl. I'm so sorry."

"Thank you, Daddy," I utter, leaning against his shoulder. "I want you home more. But I also want you to understand I'll date whoever I want. I care a lot for Daniel and I have enough stress in my life without having to fret over if you approve of him or not."

Everyone grows quiet and it's Daniel who breaks the silence.

"I won't ever hurt her. Never," Daniel assures them. "Lauren deserves all the love in the world, and I'm just one part of her world. We don't have to be divided here. Each of us wants the same thing: Lauren's happiness."

Dad's shoulders relax and he shoots Landon a look. Those two often talk silently, sharing the same brain. Landon walks over and ruffles my hair.

"I'm cool if Laur has a sugar daddy." He shrugs. "I'm off to see my girl. See you guys later."

I mouth a thank you to my brother.

"I'm not her sugar daddy," Daniel clarifies, making me snort with laughter.

"Thank fuck, because I was about to beat your ass," Dad grumbles.

I can't help but giggle, which makes both my guys smile. If Mom were here, she'd wink at me. We'd share our own silent conversation, one that says we know just how to bring the men in our world to their knees. God, I miss her.

Normally, thinking of Mom brings down my mood. But when your mood is as low as it can go, I can only go up from here. Mom was a fighter.

I'm a fighter too.

Fire burns in my stomach as newfound determination thrums through my veins.

So my kidneys are crapping out on me. That sucks. Really fucking sucks. But it's not the end of the world. Not yet. I won't let it be. I'm going to learn what I can, get the help I need, and fight for the life I deserve.

Happiness.

It's mine. I just have to fight for it.

"Did you come here straight from work?" I ask, chewing on a piece of chicken.

He nods as he makes a sandwich. "You weren't answering and it was worrying me."

Guilt trickles through me. These people worry about my health and it's unfair to leave them hanging. I vow to do better and not purposefully scare them if I can help it.

"I'm sorry," I tell him, sipping on some ice water. "I was in a dark place."

He cuts his sandwich in half and then comes to sit beside me at the kitchen table. After a stern talking to from Dad about "no hanky-panky in his house," Dad retired to his room, giving Daniel and me some privacy.

"Want to talk about it?" he asks as he practically

inhales his food. I know today was a long shift and it makes me wonder how long he's gone without eating. His dedication to his job is admirable. It's doctors like him who help people like me. They care and want solutions. They want to heal and cure. They give hope.

"Missing my mom and worrying over things," I admit. "I should have replied. Honestly, I was too exhausted. All cried out."

He swallows and darts his eyes to my plate, silently indicating I should continue eating. "We all have bad days, angel. You're allowed them."

I eat a cooked carrot and shake my head. "Normal people, yes. Me, no. I can't afford bad days. They all need to count. Every day has to be a good one."

"This isn't Instagram," he says grumpily. "You can't just show people all the good and expect that to accurately portray your life."

"No, I agree. I'm not hiding anymore. But I'm also not going to fall into the pit of despair. Mom would want me to take my life by the horns and ride with everything I've got."

He lifts a brow, smirking. "Of all the analogies, you choose the dirtiest one."

A laugh bubbles up my throat. "You're just horny if bull riding gets you hot."

"You get me hot," he says, flashing me a flirty grin.

My heart does a flop in my chest and my skin heats. Daniel is good for me. He helps me forget all the wrongs because he's so damn right.

"Dad said nothing about the porch," I tease, stabbing at another carrot and licking it.

His green eyes burn hot. "You're not riding me on your father's porch."

I give him a faux pout, batting my lashes. "I guess I'll have to settle for sucking your dick instead."

He leans forward, gently gripping my neck. I'm pulled right into a possessive kiss that makes my stomach tighten with anticipation. "Naughty angel."

"You like it."

"No," he growls. "I love it. A little too much, in fact. I'm going to have to walk through your house with a damn hard-on."

"Which I could take care of on the porch," I remind him.

"How about you kiss me like you mean it and then I'll take you to my house tomorrow night, cook you dinner, and then take care of you on my bed."

"So I'm dessert, huh?"

"It's only fair since I'm a…what did you call it? That's right. I'm a snack."

I bark out a laugh. "Damn right. A yummy little snack."

His dark brow hikes up. "Little, huh?"

"I mean, I could disprove this myth…on the porch."

"Bad girl," he growls.

He likes it when I'm bad.

CHAPTER
thirteen

Daniel

Three weeks later...

"**Y**ou look nervous," I say as I guide Lauren into my house.

She frowns. "I'm officially meeting your daughter for the first time as your girlfriend. What if she kicks my ass?"

The idea of Jenna kicking anyone's ass is cute. She's tiny and has a fierce scowl, but she wouldn't hurt a fly.

"This is a happy home," I tease. "No ass whippings." Then I lean in while grabbing her ass. "Unless you're into it later."

She snorts. "Oh, I'll be into it."

Things feel lighter than they have been, which is nice. Teddy tolerates me and Landon actually likes me. Her family isn't the problem, though. It's her. Well, her body specifically. She went to her specialist, Dr. Benton, and what we feared is true. Her right kidney is overrun by cysts, many of them on the brink of rupturing. At this point, she doesn't need dialysis, but it's coming. Frequent kidney infections and continual pain in her abdomen is the norm for her. All we can do is treat the symptoms and try to prevent things from worsening.

Sometimes, it's so fucking hard to be her boyfriend when I crave to doctor the hell out of her. I just want her—need her—to be okay. Dr. Benton said that often, people with ADPKD, will end up needing a transplant. Scary as hell because it makes me think about losing her, which is unimaginable. After he dropped that bomb, I took her home and held her while she cried.

She hasn't cried much since.

That's one beautiful thing about Lauren…she may feel defeated, but she never gives up.

Lauren is a fighter.

"Yum," Lauren says as we enter my kitchen where Enzo is already hard at work over the stove. Enzo, an Italian social worker and my daughter's husband, stirs something in a pot.

"My mother's chicken parmesan recipe," he says over his shoulder. "It's been modified a bit." Spaghetti squash rather than regular noodles, no added salt, and sugar-free sauce. We discussed what he was going to cook prior to her coming over so I could make sure she could eat it.

I give him a thankful nod of my head. Because of Lauren's condition, she's to decrease her salt and protein intake. With those notes, Enzo has taken it upon himself to cook the family something that will be good for her as well. Most guys wouldn't like that their son-in-law lives with them, but our situation is different. And temporary.

"Where are my girls?" I ask as I usher Lauren to a bar stool.

"Jenna and Cora went out back to see if there were any cherry tomatoes growing on the vines for the salad." He places a lid on the pot and then strides over to Lauren. "Enzo. Nice to meet you."

Her cheeks turn slightly pink and I suppress a grin. Enzo is the typical Italian good-looking man. I've seen women do double takes at him, and Lauren is no different. I'll just tease her about it later.

"Lauren," she greets, shaking his hand. "Thanks for cooking. That's really sweet of you."

"Anything for my old man," he jokes, ribbing me in the side.

In truth, I'm not much older than the guy.

"PopPop!"

Cora hugs my leg and I reach down to stroke her hair. I'm technically her guardian—on paper—but Jenna is every bit her mother where it counts. I scoop up my *granddaughter* and kiss her adorable face.

"Hi, Cora Bug. Did you get some tomatoes?"

She holds out one of her fists, red juice running down her wrist. "Mato, PopPop!"

I pretend to try and eat her fist, making her squeal.

"Hey, Dad. Hi, Lauren," Jenna says, coming to stand beside me. She leans her head on my shoulder. "I'm starving."

Lauren's stiff posture relaxes. I think she expected war, kind of like the first time I met her family. But my family is easygoing.

"It smells amazing," Lauren says. "If it's as good as it smells, I'll take a picture and post about it on my blog."

"You have a blog?" Jenna asks. "About what?"

Lauren shrugs. "Food. Books. Sunsets."

"Sounds fun," Jenna says, smiling. "I'll have to check it out."

"Sometimes I interview hot doctors," Lauren reveals.

"Oh yeah? Dad on there?"

"No, but George Clooney is."

I snort. "This one's a snarky smartass," I tell Jenna. "Aren't you, angel?"

"I have no idea what you're talking about," Lauren says, blinking her big brown eyes in an innocent way.

Jenna laughs, which makes Cora giggle. Cute little Cora never knows what she's laughing at...she just loves to do it.

"At least we know these two will get along," Enzo says, ruffling Jenna's hair and messing it up. "They're both brats."

The movie has long since ended. Enzo already carried Jenna off to bed, promising to be back to fetch Cora. I can't help but smile at Lauren and Cora. Lauren has drifted off and has a sleeping three-year-old glued to her side. With Cora's blond hair nearly the color of Lauren's, they could almost pass for mother and daughter. Since I never saw my own daughter at this age, loss pangs in my heart. I missed out on so much. Maybe one day I'll get to do the whole parenting thing again, but not from age eighteen and on. From birth would be fantastic.

I feel Lauren's sleepy eyes on me and I flick my gaze to hers. Her fingers stroke through Cora's hair as she burns me with an intense stare.

"I'll never have kids," she tells me, seemingly reading my thoughts.

All I can do is frown.

"Not that I don't want to have them, because I do, but because it would be irresponsible of me." Her eyes water. "I've been reading up on ADPKD, and my kind is most definitely hereditary. If there's a chance I could pass it on, I don't want to take it."

My heart clenches. I hate that Lauren will never have a normal life. That she'll never be able to do the things any other woman her age can do for fear of it impacting her health or someone else's. She can't even eat regular spaghetti, for fuck's sake. Rather than placate her and give her false hope, I reach forward and squeeze her thigh.

"You're the strongest woman I know," I tell her firmly.

Her features relax and she smiles. "Thank you for being exactly the man I need."

Enzo walks back into the media room and scoops Cora up. He winks at me before disappearing.

"Come on," I tell Lauren, rising from the sofa to pull her up. "You're staying here tonight."

She smirks. "Is that so?"

"Yep. Get used to it."

I hug her to me, tugging on her hair so she's forced to look up. A serene smile plays at her lips. Leaning forward, I kiss her softly. When I pull away, I quickly asses her. She's tired. Feeling unwell. It's written all over her face—dark circles under eyes, ashen skin, slumped shoulders.

"Let's get you to bed," I say, grabbing her ass and lifting her.

She holds on and doesn't even fight me when I take her straight to bed. So she can sleep. No fucking. It's days like these that scare the shit out of me.

∾

I scrub my hands with soap and then rinse them off before drying them on a paper towel. I'm tired as hell. Thank fuck it's nearly time to go.

"You heading out, Dr. Venable?" Lin asks as she scribbles something on a chart.

"I have to finish writing up something for Dr. Morris, but then I'll be leaving. I'll be in my office if you need me."

She waves to me as I stride down the hall. Once I push through the door of my small office, I freeze at seeing Lauren there. Her back is to me as she stares at a painting on the wall. I appreciate her delicate, feminine form. In just a simple yellow dress and white wedge heels, she's fucking stunning. Upon realizing my presence, she turns her head, her brown eyes darting my way.

Troubled.

Upset.

Angry.

I see it all flash across her face before she masks it away, giving me her flirtiest smile. With confidence, she struts over to me and grabs onto either side of my stethoscope hanging around my neck.

"Wanna play doctor, Dr. Dan?"

No. I want to know what the fuck is wrong with her.

"Lauren—"

She presses her palm to my mouth, her eyes closing briefly. "I just need you. Right now. Can you give that to me, Daniel? Please? I promise, you can play real doctor in five minutes. But right now, I need the dirty, filthy you. I need to forget about my life and focus on us."

I grip her wrist and pull her hand from my

mouth. "Five minutes. It's like you don't even know me. I'll need at least seven minutes."

This makes her laugh and it's so fucking pretty.

"Thank you," she says. "Now close the door. Lock it too. We don't need any naughty nurses peeking in on your sexy doctor ass."

I close the door and lock it. "Any more demands, angel?"

"Sit down in your chair. I want to fuck you on it."

My dick is hard and threatening to rip through my scrubs. I pull out my keys and toss them to her. "My wallet is in that cabinet. Grab us a condom."

I sit down in my chair and stalk her with my eyes as she sashays over to the cabinet. She looks over her shoulder at me, teasing me as she lifts her dress some. Then, she turns back to her task of finding my wallet. Once she has the condom, she prances over to me, standing between my spread thighs.

"Open your mouth," she instructs.

I part my lips. She makes me hold the condom between my teeth. My brow arches as if to ask, "What's next?"

"First," she purrs, like she's giving me a lesson. "I'm going to need you to get me nice and wet, Dr. Dan."

She lifts her leg and rests her foot on the armrest of my chair. Her dress hides what's beneath. I give her a wicked grin as I pull the condom from my mouth.

"I'm going to need my mouth," I say as I toss the

condom on the desk. "You just stay there like a good girl. I'll take care of you, honey."

I lift her dress and groan to discover she isn't wearing panties. Letting the dress fall over my head, hiding me, I seek out her cunt that smells delicious with her arousal. She lets out a small moan when I tease along her slit with the tip of my finger, reveling in the wet evidence I find there. Back and forth. Back and forth. I rub at her, slowly and expertly, until she's trembling. And I haven't even touched her clit yet.

Something's wrong and she's upset, but we'll get to that. I just want to gift her a few minutes of escape. Of peace. Of us. For now, I want to make her forget. Flicking my tongue out, I tease at her tiny nub between her pussy lips. Her breath is sharp and she grips onto my hair, messing it up.

"Oh, God," she breathes.

I smile and then suck on her clit. My finger slides easily inside her tight depths. Slowly, I fingerfuck the girl of my dreams as she dances on my tongue. If it were up to me, I'd keep her on the edge of pleasure forever, suspended in a time where everything in our world is paused and perfect. But her body, per usual, does as it wants. She explodes with a loud whimper, her body trembling with release.

Pulling out from under her dress, I slip my finger from her and then flash her an innocent grin. "Having fun up there?"

Her cheeks are pink and she seems dazed. "It'd be more fun down there."

"Put a condom on me, angel, and you can have all the fun you want."

She picks up the condom as I pull my scrubs down enough to free my cock. It juts proudly at her, waiting for attention. Her smirk is nearly my undoing as she rips open the foil packet. With dainty, but sure hands, she rolls the condom down my length. Brown eyes find mine and lock there as she climbs on my lap, straddling me. She reaches under her dress to find my cock. We both hiss out when she sinks down over my length, fully seating herself on me.

Then she crumbles.

My strong, beautiful girl breaks apart.

I hold her to me as she cries against my neck. Every cell inside my body explodes with dread. Gently, I stroke her soft blond hair and offer caresses meant to soothe the girl I love.

And I do love her.

Wildly and without regret.

When love feels limited, it rushes out fast and hard like a damn geyser. Powerful and unstoppable. But geysers eventually stop. And that's what scares me.

I want her to tell me what's wrong, but she doesn't. She kisses my neck, her tears soaking me, as she works her hips. Up and down. Up and down. This is what she wants—needs—and I'll give it to her. Even if it kills me to have her like this.

Pressing my lips to her hair, I whisper the words that are probably inappropriate and too soon, but words she needs to hear nonetheless. "I love you, angel."

"I love you too," she breathes against my neck. Hot and unapologetic.

Gripping her hair, I pull her mouth to mine. I kiss her deeply as though I have the power to climb inside her and touch her flickering soul. As though I have the ability to heal it with just a kiss. I'll damn sure try.

She works me good with her expert movements until I'm groaning out my release. Her body doesn't slow until she's sure I'm done. Then, she collapses against me, exhausted and spent.

"Best four minutes of my life," she jokes. I hear truth in them too.

"At least seven minutes, angel. Get your facts straight."

"Little liar who lies," she mutters, pulling away to look at me, the grin quickly falling from her pretty lips. "I start dialysis next week."

With my softening dick inside her and our heart-felt proclamations of love still lingering in the air, my girlfriend tells me we've just moved to the next level. And it has nothing to do with our relationship.

"I love you," I whisper.

It's the only words I can say.

I'll say them as many times as I possibly can, be-cause time feels limited and finite.

Fuck time.

CHAPTER
fourteen

Lauren

Six months later...

"**G**o fish," I tell Taylor, a little blond-haired boy with big green eyes.

He taps a button on his iPad and squeals. I glance down at my iPad, groaning to see he's just "got his wish."

"Boooo," I gripe. "You always win."

"'Cause I'm the best fisher, Lo-Lo," he says, grinning.

He's in the next station over. We can look at each other, but aren't close enough to touch. If we were, I'd give him a big hug. I love that kid. For being eleven and requiring dialysis already, he's such a trooper. We're always scheduled at the same times on the same days. He's my little buddy.

"Fine, you're the best," I concede. "Want to play another round or is your famous YouTuber more exciting than me?"

"He just put out a new Fortnite video," he explains, pulling his headphones up to his ears. "I can't miss it."

I playfully stick out my tongue. I'm in dire need of studying anyway. College is hard, especially with so many hours a week spent at this hell hole, but I love it anyway. I quickly lose myself in my English assignment, wondering how this stuff will even help me when I become a therapist one day.

Mom would be so proud. I know Dad is. And Daniel is just excited that I've made a plan, rather than wallowing in despair. It gives me something to focus on, so I don't focus on the crappy parts of my life.

Even when I'm having my worst day, I realize it could always be worse. Like Taylor, for instance. He's parentless. Was living with his aunt when his mom died, but then his aunt decided to drown out her stress with a bottle of pills. Went to sleep and never woke up. He's lost the people he loved to death and now lives in a foster home.

When I go home each night, my dad is there. No more overnight or weekend trips. He was true to his word, staying in town for work. And even though Landon moved out with Callie, they're home all the time visiting and eating up Dad's food because they're poor. I have a dad and brother who care about me. Taylor has no one.

This is one of the reasons I want to be a therapist. I want to know how people handle the shit in their lives and be able to help them handle it better. People like Taylor need to talk out their feelings.

Behind his big green eyes is heartbreak that he hides with silly smiles. He's like me, and maybe that's why I recognize it so easily.

"It's so quiet in here," a deep voice booms, warming me to my core. "Did you bore Taylor to the point he's ignoring you now?"

Taylor snorts and waves to Daniel.

"No, brat," I grumble. "A new YouTuber video."

"So that's what we're calling it," he says to Taylor, winking in exaggeration. As though he really just needed an escape from me.

"Don't you have bedpans to clean out?" I bite back.

Daniel, amused at my grumpiness, saunters into the room. He pulls out a sucker and hands it to Taylor before walking over to me. I'm given a root beer one since those are my favorites.

"You can't woo me with candy," I lie. He totally can and does it all the time.

"I better take it back then," he teases.

I snatch the sucker and stuff it into my purse. "Are you on break?"

When I started dialysis, I had a choice between three places and the hospital. I chose the hospital so Daniel would be accessible. Sometimes, when we're super bored, he'll hang out with Taylor and me to help pass the time.

"I'm off early. Thought maybe we could go to that bookshop you love. Maybe even visit Aiden's restaurant for some dinner." He sits in the chair beside me and wraps an arm around me. "I missed you."

I lean against him and relax. "Missed you too."

"Are you feeling up to it?"

Truth is, I'm tired today. Groggy and weak. Crabby.

But I feel like that just about every day, so I grin it and bear it like usual.

"How about we save the bookshop for another day and just hit Aiden's instead?"

Daniel, always the perceptive one, assesses my features and gives me a nod. "Perfect."

My chest aches and I feel hollow. We're as perfect as we can be without my deteriorating body putting a damper on things. I wish our lives were easier for us. When I feel eyes on me, I catch Taylor watching us.

Longing.

Sadness.

Emptiness.

I offer him a bright smile. It could always be worse. Taylor, of all people, knows this.

Thankfully, he smiles back.

$\sim$

"You're off. Everything okay?" Daniel asks, walking out of his bathroom looking like a tasty daddy snack in his flannel pajama pants.

"It is now," I say, biting on my bottom lip and waggling my brows at him suggestively.

He laughs. "You can't fool me, pervert."

I pretend to be annoyed at his words, but the moment he curls up beside me and wraps a possessive arm around me, I forget how to be mad. In his arms, I'm happy. Loved. Secure.

"You remember how I said I don't want to have kids?" I say against his chest, running my fingertips along the grooves.

"I do."

"Well, I haven't proposed yet, sheesh," I tease.

He chuckles. "You're extra silly when you're stressed. Why don't you tell me what's bothering you?"

I let out a heavy sigh. "I meant physically. But I still want to be a mom one day, you know?" I tilt my head up to look at him.

"You know I'll give you whatever makes you happy," he says, his green eyes burning with intensity. "Anything."

"Anything?"

"Anything."

"I want your cock then." It's not a lie, it's just not the actual thing I was thinking about. I want a family. Him. A future.

"I'll give you my cock first. Then I'll give you the rest."

Sometimes it freaks me out how well he can read me.

Mostly, I'm just extremely thankful.

Oh God.

Oh God.

Tears burn like acid down my temples as I writhe on the bed. Sometimes, the pain is too intense. The stupid rupturing cysts and chronic kidney infections are killing me. Pun intended. I can't even laugh at my own joke because a sob chases it away. I'm drenched in sweat, but I'm also cold. My eyes are squeezed shut so tight, I have no idea what time of day it is or anything.

I need to call Daniel.

Or Dad.

Or Landon.

I need someone.

Sucking in a harsh breath, I pry a hand away from my aching abdomen and pat around the bed on a hunt for my phone. I squint at the bright screen, trying to make sense of it, but the blinding headache throbbing in my skull makes it difficult. Bile rises in my throat and I swallow it down. I don't have the energy or strength to crawl out of this bed and into the bathroom.

The phone slips from my grip when another wave of pain assaults me. All I can do is sob for my mommy. If she were here, she'd know just what to do. Moms are amazing like that. Everyone should have a mom like I had. This makes me cry harder. It also makes me think about other people who don't have moms. People like Taylor. Life is a cruel sonofabitch. Yeah, life's totally a man, because it's the one doing all the fucking around here.

"Lauren," Dad's voice booms out, echoing inside my head.

"Daddy," I whimper. "It hurts."

"Shhh, baby girl," he coos, his palm going to my forehead. "I'm going to get you to the hospital. Want me to call Daniel too or is he there?"

I don't know.

I don't know anything.

A wave of nausea hits and I puke all over my poor father.

Sorry, Daddy.

"Hi, Lauren," a man greets. "I'm Wendell. How are you feeling?"

I blink at an unfamiliar man.

"Where am I?" I croak.

"In the ambulance," Dad says from the other side.

"Why?"

"Figured you'd like to ride in style," Wendell offers.

I fade in and out of consciousness. Everything is a blur of activity when I make it to the hospital.

Dad goes missing. I cry. Just when I think I've been abandoned, my favorite doctor strides in, worry contorting his handsome face.

He's shouting orders and it feels too loud. The lights and sounds and everything. I just want it all to go away.

And then it does.

Poof.

CHAPTER
fifteen

Daniel

I'm damn near climbing the walls, desperate to go into the operating room and check on things, but I know Dr. Cohen needs focus. Rushing into the OR freaking the fuck out is not going to help.

"Drink this," Morris says, thrusting a water bottle at me.

My hand shakes as I snag it and chug down half the contents. "How are Teddy and Landon?"

"Good as can be expected."

I scrub my palm down my face. "Jenna here?"

"She is. Enzo and Cora stayed home."

"You think everything's okay?" I ask, chancing a look at my friend.

His lips purse together, making my heart sink. "Aneurysms are no joke," he says sadly. "But you saw the scans. If they can get on top of it, she'll be fine."

I glance at the clock. She's been in there for a while. Had the aneurysm burst, she would've died on the table.

"Breathe, man," Morris says, gripping my shoulder.

A sharp breath escapes me. "Coil embolization. It's a successful treatment plan. It will work."

He nods as though he believes me.

Fuck, I barely believe myself.

"Sit the hell down in your office and take a breather. I'll bring some of those vanilla cookies you love," he says, grabbing my other shoulder to walk me away from the OR.

I skid to a halt. "I can't. What if...what if..."

What if she dies?

What if they need me?

"Fine, then at least sit. You're wearing a hole in this gorgeous linoleum. The hospital has had it since the '60s. That shit is irreplaceable."

I let out a small laugh, thankful for his ability to lighten any dark situation.

A door opens and Nurse Eleanor exits the OR.

"Dr. Venable," she calls out.

I stalk over to her, my heart dropping with every step. "Yes." My voice is a husky croak. Morris is right at my side for moral support.

"Dr. Cohen asked me to step out and inform you that the coil embolization was successful. She'll need to frequently have it monitored, but she should be okay."

Her words sink in my bones, burrowing there.

She should be okay.

It was successful.

My legs shake with the urge to fall to my knees

and sob in fucking relief. But I can't do that. I have a family to talk to.

Mine.

∽

Two weeks later...

"No. No. No." Lauren flips through the Netflix shows past all the ones we've seen. She's restless and agitated.

"What about that one?" I ask, pointing absently.

As she reads the description, I crawl into my bed and stare at her. Even weak and tired, she's beautiful. The aneurism was just one of her problems. Her cysts on her right kidney have grown in size and two had ruptured. So on top of everything, she's been in severe pain. And, because of the excessive bleeding and eventual clot formation, she developed a urinary tract infection. My girl gets delivered blow after blow.

"Maybe I'll just go to bed," she says grumpily, tossing the remote.

Her anger and irritation barely hides the tears brimming.

"Want to talk about it?"

She hisses, the tears leaking out. "What's there to talk about? My body hates me."

I reach up and brush away a tear with my thumb before kissing her forehead. "We could talk about that terrible robe my mother brought over for you to wear."

Despite her trying to remain in a bad mood, her lips twitch. "It's a lovely shade of baby shit green. Like your eyes." She bats her lashes at me.

I snort. "Maybe I should tell Mom that since she has the same eye color as me."

"Your mother will never believe it. She loves me," she brags.

Lauren may be joking, but it's true. They finally met after I brought Lauren to my house once she was discharged from the hospital. Mom stayed for a few days cooking and cleaning. It was strained at first because my mother wasn't keen on the age gap, but all it took was being around us for a full day to understand how much love we have for each other. Once she realized I was happy and that Lauren was it for me, she relaxed and let my girl in her heart too.

My girl never leaves once she roots herself in there.

"Tomorrow you want to get out of the house and go to that bookshop?" I suggest. I know she's tired and hurting, but it's something she can do. Sitting inside the house alone while I work is not good for her. She needs fresh air.

"I'd like that," she whispers. "Maybe recreate our first date."

Minus the wild fucking and subsequent ER visit.

"We could have sex," she says, reading my mind.

"Or we could do more of this." I brush her hair from her face and kiss her deeply. "You like this?"

Her fingers thread in my hair as she pulls me closer. "I really like this."

Our lips dance together frantically since her body isn't able to join in on the party. One day it'll be ready again, and I'll be ready too. Until then, kissing is perfectly fine by me. Hell, staring at her as she lives and fucking breathes would be okay too. With Lauren, I'll take whatever I can get.

～

She flips the page on her book slowly, her eyebrows furrowed in concentration. I watch her from across the coffee table where I sit in my armchair. The bookshop is quiet on this cold, snowy day. I could stare at the snow falling down outside, or I could stare at her.

I'll always choose her.

Another page flip.

And another.

I'm glad for the day off to spend it doing nothing with her. Outside of the house. She needs a break from the medicine, her illness, life.

Another page flip.

Absently, she reaches for her bottle of water, but she's too engrossed in her book to realize she's nowhere near it. I lean forward, unscrew the lid, and hand it to her. She sips it and then hands it back.

Her hair is messy from having air dried and been pulled into a bun. Dark circles paint her cheeks under her eyes and her skin is pallid. Even her full, pink lips are dry and cracked.

But she's alive.

Still fucking here.

My fighter.

Lauren Englewood.

It's then I imagine her as something else. Mine. Lauren Venable. The thought sends my heart galloping in my chest. I try to envision her in a white gown walking down the aisle in front of hundreds of people. But it doesn't feel right. Instead, I think of the cabin on the lake I sometimes rent from my friend Dane. How even when it's snowy, the lake is beautiful.

I love Lauren and can't imagine life without her.

So what am I waiting for?

"I'll be right back," I tell her. "You'll be okay for a little while?"

"Mmmhmm," she murmurs without looking up.

I chuckle and kiss the top of her head. "Text me if you need me."

Quickly, I tug on my coat and gloves before heading outside in the blistery cold. Where I'm going, I won't need a car. I walk a block down to the nearest jewelry store. Once inside, the woman at the counter, who looks to be around my mother's age, brightens at seeing me.

"Good evening, sir. What can I help you with?"

I give her a sheepish grin. "I'm looking for a ring. For my girl."

Her eyes glitter with excitement. "What kind of ring?"

"One that says I'll love you forever, no matter how long that may be."

"Ahh, a romantic looking to propose?"

"Yeah."

"What kind of budget are we looking at?" she asks as she walks me over to a glass case.

"I'll just know it when I see it."

I peer into the case and peruse all the sparkly diamonds. They all look the same to me. Until I find the one that stands out. A giant yellow diamond surrounded by mandarin garnets and then another circle of rubies. It reminds me of a sunset. So Lauren.

"That one," I say, pointing at it.

"That one's the priciest in the bunch," she warns.

I glance at her name tag. "Can you put a price tag on love, Wanda?"

Her eyes gleam. "Certainly not, Mr. um…"

"Dr. Venable is fine."

"I'll wrap this up, Doctor."

∞

The snow is growing heavier and the wind blows hard, but I'm stunned as I stare at her through the window.

Her smile is wide and bright as she talks to a child no older than five or six. The child wears a white plastic helmet and seems bashful, but is also smiling. It's no different than how she lights up Taylor's face at the hospital or even Cora's.

She does this to people.

Lauren may love sunsets, but she's the sunrise, lifting high above everyone and giving them something to look up to. She warms them with her smiles and reflects back hope.

As I walk back inside, the woman with the child is walking out. I recognize her. Another foster parent like myself. I'd gotten into the gig because of wanting to help Jenna get Cora, but I've gotten to know some of the locals around here through the meetings and online forums.

"Anna? How's it going?"

Anna smiles. "Just picking up a book for Ollie. He just joined us."

I squat down and retrieve a sucker from my pocket. "I'm Dr. Venable. Want a sucker?"

Ollie looks up at Anna and she nods.

"Ollie is a cool name," I tell him. "Where'd you get the cool hat?"

His dark eyes brighten. "You like it?"

"Pretty cool if you ask me. I'm a doctor and see them all the time, but this is the coolest one I've ever seen," I assure him.

"Why?" he asks.

"Because it's sitting on the head of a cool little guy, duh."

He giggles. "That lady said it looks like a dinosaur egg."

"Are you a dinosaur?" I tease.

The boy nods. "Rawwwr."

"Dinosaurs usually get extra hungry and sometimes need two suckers. Don't you think?"

He beams at me. "They do!"

When I stand and hand him another, I nod at Anna. "Be careful out there. It's slick."

"Thanks, Dr. Venable," Ollie says, waving his two suckers at me.

They head out of the store and I find Lauren still in her chair. She's no longer engrossed in a book, but her attention is fully on me. I love the look on her face so much that I can't even wait another moment to make this perfect or thought through. I simply stalk over to her and sit on my knees in front of her. Her smile is serene as I take her hand.

"Lauren," I murmur, admiring her pretty face that can't be hidden away by fatigue and depression and disease. "I love you."

"I love you too," she says with a grin.

"So much that I want you to be my wife. Life's too precious to let moments slip by us. Will you marry me and grab all the moments with me?"

Her eyes fill with tears. "Really? You want to marry me?"

"Hell yeah I want to marry you."

"Do you even have a ring?" she challenges, her brown eyes shiny with tears but dancing with mischief.

"What do you think?"

"Holy shit, you do."

I smirk as I fish around in my pocket full of suckers. When I find the one I want, I pull it out and slide the ring over the stick before offering it to her much like I would one of my pediatric patients.

"Root beer," she croons. "You sure know the way to a girl's heart."

"To be clear, you only get the sucker if you say yes," I tease.

She slides the ring off the stick and her eyes widen. "It's so beautiful."

I pluck it out of her hand and slide it onto her ring finger. It's a little loose, but the lady assured me we could resize it if necessary.

"Will you be mine?"

"I already am."

"Is that a yes?" I confirm, smirking.

"Well, I want the sucker," she sasses. "Yes, Dr. Dan. I'll marry your handsome grandpa ass because I love you more than you'll ever know."

I slide my hands into her messy hair and pull her in for a kiss. Our kiss is a sealing of two souls. The inked stitching on my ribs seems to burn. Ripping and pulling apart. Not to get out and search for purpose or peace. No, to open up and pull her in too. She's a part of me and I'll never let her go.

CHAPTER
sixteen

Lauren

Four months later...

I will not cry. I will not cry. I will not cry.

Taylor: Are you crying?

Hastily, I swipe away the tear on my cheek as I stare at the message window on the new game Taylor and I are playing. I can feel his wide green eyes on me. Forcing a smile, I shake my head.

"Nope," I say aloud. "Just cleaning my cheeks."

He laughs. "That's a new one. I'll have to remember to use that one on Vera."

"Vera still being good to you?" I ask, no longer amused. When I'd seen a bruise on his arm last week, I nearly lost my shit in the dialysis room.

"She's fine," he says, a scowl forming. "They're always fine."

His answer digs at me. It's not fair. Not only does he have kidney disease, but he's also been forced into the system. I have a loving, supportive network of people. He has no one.

The tears fall harder this time, nothing to do with the pain I'm feeling.

"Your move," I croak, nodding at his device.

While he frowns down at the screen to focus, I stare at him. Getting adopted out of the system is already hard enough for an older child, but what about one with medical issues? That seems like it's even more impossible.

I tap out a message on our game.

Me: You think Vera will let you come to my wedding Saturday? I could see if Enzo could arrange it if you wanted to come.

He smiles broadly at me. "Really?"

"I know Enzo's not your caseworker, but he has pull. Only if you want to come, of course," I say, grinning back at him.

"I want to, Lauren!"

"Good, it's a done deal then."

"I'm glad you're marrying Dr. Dum-Dum," he says, looking back down at his game. "He always has suckers and he's nice."

"Yeah, I love Dr. Dum-Dum." I smirk because Daniel is going to love his new nickname. He had it coming always handing out Dum-Dum suckers. Joy chases away the hurt inside my body, even if only momentarily.

My eyes skim over Taylor once more. The ache inside me lives in my chest this time. Coming in here three days a week for months and months has allowed me to get to know the quiet, yet quirky kid. A yearning burns inside me unlike anything I've ever felt.

Quickly, before I lose my nerve, I text Daniel.

Me: The house is lonely lately.

Since Jenna and her family moved out, it's just Daniel. I'd been spending most of my nights with Daniel anyway, so one day Dad and Daniel brought over my stuff. I never thought I'd see the day where my dad helps my boyfriend move my things into his home. But it feels right with Daniel. I love him and I'm going to marry him, for Pete's sake. Now that my pictures of my family sit on my bedside table and I get to curl up to my fiancé every night, a certain level of peace has entered my world.

Daniel: I miss Cora too.

She belongs with her family, but I know it hurt Daniel to see her go.

Me: Ever think about fostering anyone else?

Daniel: Like a certain green-eyed boy?

My heart flutters in my chest. Of course he'd be able to read me like no one else.

Me: I mean, I'd be the favorite of course. He calls you Dr. Dum-Dum...

A smile tugs at my lips.

Daniel: You're everyone's favorite. Maybe I should carry around Smarties instead...

God, I love this man.

Me: Dum-Dums are SO you though.

Daniel: Yes.

Me: Yes, you're a Dum-Dum?

Daniel: Yes, to Taylor. Let's do this.

I feel as though my heart stops completely in my chest. My tears blur and race down my hot cheeks, this time with a happier emotion.

Me: I love you, Dr. Dum-Dum.

Most women don't throw up on their wedding day. I'm not most women. Everything in my life happens at the most inopportune times and with the force of a hurricane. Could I not just have one day where I felt great? One day.

My stomach heaves and tears leak out ruining all Jenna's hard work on my makeup. I miss Mom. She'd be here to hold back my hair and promise me everything would be okay. Someone knocks on the bathroom door at the tiny cabin we're at.

"Everything okay in there?"

Dad.

"I'm fine," I croak out. A big fat lie.

"I'm your dad, remember? I know when you lie, baby girl."

Since the bathroom is so small, I shakily reach over and unlock the door. Dad, looking handsome as ever in a suit, slides inside and crouches beside me. His fingers stroke through my hair.

"Do I need to get Daniel?" Worry flashes in his eyes.

"No," I say in vehemence. "Today he's going to

be my husband. I'd rather not walk down the aisle with him in doctor mode."

Dad's lips purse together, but he doesn't argue. Instead, he pulls open a cabinet door under the sink and grabs a rag. Once he's wet it with cold water and wrung it out, he kneels again beside me. He's gentle as he cleans the vomit from my lips. Mom was always the one who dealt with puke when we were kids. Always. But now that she's gone, Dad has stepped up in all ways.

"I love you, Daddy," I blurt out, tears once again filling my eyes.

"I love you too," he assures me. "I know today is hard on you because of losing Mom, but you know she's looking down on you. She'd be so proud, Lauren. I know I am."

I scoff. "Proud of what? Me sitting on the bathroom floor as I puke my guts out because my body is deteriorating?"

Undeterred, he chuckles and sits down, taking my hand. "No, I'm proud that despite everything you're going through, you still have your fire. That you can crack jokes at the worst possible times and that you've managed to find love during the sickest part of your life. That you are going to college, taking a stab at a future you deserve. It's admirable and brave. Lots of people would want to give up or give in to depression. Not my fiery little girl. You're a force, Lauren. Don't ever forget that."

On the floor, weak and nauseous and in pain, I feel anything but strong.

Dad stares at me with conviction in his eyes. The same way Daniel looks at me. They see someone much stronger than who I see in the mirror every day.

"Some days I feel like it's too hard," I admit, my voice cracking.

"And some days it is. Today being one of them. But you have to be harder and tougher. Are you going to let this disease own you on your wedding day?"

"Hell no," I tell him, already feeling better with encouragement flowing through my veins.

"That's my girl. Now, take a breather and then clean your mouth before you kiss your husband." He laughs. "Or not. I mean, for better or worse, am I right?"

A giggle erupts from me. I definitely got Dad's sense of humor. "Daniel has seen a lot with me, but even that would be a new one for us."

Dad shrugs. "It could be poetic justice for him swooping in and taking my baby girl. Just sayin'."

"Go away," I playfully grumble.

He helps me to my feet and flushes the toilet. Dad roots around in the drawers until he finds an unopened toothbrush. I set to brushing my teeth while Dad watches me in the mirror. It reminds me of when I was a little girl all dressed up in one of

Mom's dresses pretending to be grown. He'd always look at me with such pride in his eyes. Even now. Even with my body failing me. Once I finish brushing my teeth and fix my makeup, I turn to my dad and hug him.

"Thank you," I murmur, closing my eyes. "I needed a pep talk."

He squeezes me. "That's what dads are for, baby girl. Now get out there and marry that old man."

I snort. "Dad!"

"The grandpa jokes will never get...wait for it....*old*."

"You're a dork."

"So are you."

"I love you, Daddy."

"Love you too, sweetheart."

⌒

The cool spring air nips at my exposed flesh. If it were up to Daniel, he would've married me the day after he proposed, but when he mentioned the lake, I knew I wanted to be married here. Not with it snowing, though. No, I wanted to get married just as the sun slides down along the horizon, glimmering off the lake. I wanted Mom to be there and that felt like the closest thing. Waiting was hard, but it gave us time to plan things better.

Music plays softly, barely heard over the

cadence of the crickets chirping in the grass nearby. Today, the lake is calm and undisturbed. With a group of our closest friends and family, it's a perfect wedding day. My eyes catch the front row where Taylor sits beside Enzo. I was thrilled when he was able to make that happen. But it's the groom, though, that I can't keep my eyes off of.

Tall, strong, incredibly handsome. Daniel is all man and delicious in a suit. It's his bright smile that lights my soul on fire. His bright green eyes that shine only for me.

"Ready, baby girl?" Dad asks as he slowly guides me forward.

"Very much so."

I clutch onto my bouquet of flowers that smell fragrant and sweet. Everyone smiles proudly at us. At the end of the aisle, beside Daniel, Landon smirks at me. I guess I'll be doing the same for him in a few months when he and Callie tie the knot.

As soon as Dad passes me off to Daniel, my heart rate calms and the world seems to stop around me. The sunset is our backdrop and it couldn't be any more perfect.

"You look extra beautiful when you're about to be mine," Daniel says, leaning in to brush his lips across the shell of my ear.

"And what about after?" I sass, my voice only slightly shaking.

"It'll hurt to look at you, angel."

My heart melts. "Hope you like pain because once you start, you don't get to stop."

"I like it all with you, Lauren. And don't worry. I'll never stop."

CHAPTER
seventeen

Daniel

Two weeks later...

W e knew this was coming. Knowing and accepting are two different things, though. I'm numb as the doctor discusses the fact that Lauren must now go on a transplant waiting list. All the risk factors involved with having a kidney transplant and everything leading up to it. Whereas I'm breaking inside, Lauren remains rigid and strong. My wife has researched all there is to know about her disease. She's handling it like a champ.

And though I'm the doctor and know a transplant is her best chance at a more normal life, the husband in me freaks the fuck out over the risks.

I can't lose her.

Not now, not ever.

"...and of course friends and family can get tested."

"W-What?" I bark out, needing him to repeat what he's said.

"Potential donors."

"Test me now," I demand.

Lauren snorts and swats at my knee. "Stop."

"You may get tested, Dr. Venable, but don't get your hopes up. A lot of things, as you know, will need to be a perfect match. And giving up an organ is a big deal."

I stand abruptly and glare at him as though he's lost his mind. "And losing one is too."

"Oh my God. Sit down," Lauren grumbles. "Do not fight with my doctor or I'll send you into the hall."

I don't sit down. All I can do is pace the floor in front of the desk, anxiety clawing at my insides.

"And if no one is a match?" Lauren asks, ever the realist.

I don't wait for that answer and stalk out of the office.

∽

In my dark kitchen, I drink shot after shot, hating the injustice of the world.

Why her?

Why bright, beautiful, fierce Lauren?

Why not my asshole neighbor or that guy who used to give me shit in college or some random criminal or fuck-up?

Why young, smart, wonderful Lauren?

Another shot. Another curse word muttered under my breath.

It's been nearly a week since the doctor started the process to put her on a transplant list. She's handling shit a lot better than I am. I'm pissed and upset that her body is literally dying and there's nothing I can do about it.

I'm. A. Fucking. Doctor.

And yet, with Lauren, I'm fucking useless.

Hot tears race down my cheeks. It's the same every night. She goes to bed and I come into the dark kitchen to curse God and the world.

Nothing changes.

My wife still has a worthless goddamn kidney that's filled with tiny bombs of pain and infection that detonate whenever they fucking please. She lives in constant pain. And to make matters worse, she is on dialysis because her kidneys can't filter out all the waste like they should. She needs a break.

I shakily pour another shot of whiskey. It doesn't matter. I can drink all I want because my organs are fucking useless to her. One simple blood test proved I'm not a match. I'd been furious at the hospital when I'd received that news. Ended up having to leave early. I've been pissed ever since.

I'm desperate to beg every goddamn person in this town to get tested, but Lauren has been adamant about me staying out of it. Apparently I'm "fucking losing it." Another hot tear leaks out and before

I can swipe it away, skinny arms wrap around my middle, hugging me from behind.

"Are you done?" she asks, her cheek pressed against my back.

"Nope," I grumble.

"Yeah, you are."

I don't argue.

"Daniel, you're done," she says, this time more firmly. "You had a week to do…this. Your week is over."

The anger that has been burning through me simmers. She's right. I've been fucking sulking but to what end? Nothing is solved.

"When are you going to let your dad and brother know?" I ask, my voice husky with emotion.

"Soon. I just wanted to have a handle on my emotions before I told them."

"Maybe one of them will be a match and—"

"Honey, stop," she whispers. "I don't want that pressure on them. On anyone."

"I feel like you're giving up," I accuse, bitterness in my tone.

"No, I'm no longer giving this disease power over my every thought and action. I'm on the transplant list and if anyone wants to get tested to see if they're a match, then so be it, but I won't pressure anyone. It's a big deal."

I twist around and cradle her cheeks in my palms. "You're a big deal, angel." My lips find hers in the dark and I kiss her like she might disappear tomorrow.

"Do you love me?" she asks, knowing full well she owns my heart and soul.

"You know I do."

"Then promise on us."

"Lauren…"

"No, do it."

I grit my teeth. "Promise what?"

"That you'll stop obsessing over this. That you'll stop being angry. That you'll move forward and help me live life to the fullest. Daniel, there are things I still want out of life. And having to worry over you as you drink yourself sick every night and rage with anger is taking up too much of our time—time we could spend on something enjoyable." She runs her palms up my chest. "Let's have a cookout. Invite everyone over. Get inflatables for the kids to play in. I want to just be surrounded by family and have fun. Can we do that?"

"We can do whatever makes you happy," I concede.

"Now we're talking," she says in a teasing voice. "Before we plan a killer barbeque, I was hoping you'd take me upstairs and make love to me."

My hands find her hips, gripping her gently. "How are you feeling?"

"Good enough for my normally reserved husband to fuck me a little wild while the whiskey's still running hot through his veins."

"Reserved, huh?" I growl, nipping at her lip.

"Oh yeah," she taunts. "A real snooze-fest in the bedroom."

I grab her ass, picking her up, loving the care-free squeal she lets loose. "I better hurry and show you my animal side before I go back to hibernating bear."

She giggles as I carry her through the house. Her fingers run through my hair, caressing me. I fucking love her so much it hurts sometimes. When we make it to our bedroom, I waste no time stripping her down and laying her down on the bed. As I tear away my own clothes, I keep my gaze fixated on her perfect form. Perfect to me.

In actuality she's pale and bony. Her stomach is always swollen. Bruises constantly mar her flesh from blood tests. In her forearm, not long after she started dialysis, she was given an arteriovenous fistula—essentially permanent vascular access.

She's sick.

No denying that.

But she's also funny and fierce and gorgeous. Even at her worst, she's the best thing I've ever laid eyes on.

"The bear is hungry," she teases, her eyes alight with mischief.

She's also tired and weak.

Barely hanging on by a thread.

As much as I want to bury my face between

her thighs and drag our lovemaking on for hours, I know better. Tonight is not that night.

"Want a back rub?" I offer as I stroke my dick, staring at her.

"Oh, no, buddy. You're not playing the good doctor now. Not after that meltdown in the kitchen. Suit up and put that dick inside me."

I smirk as I grab a condom. Tearing the foil with my teeth, I then pull out the rubber and roll it on. She pushes harder to be intimate and I think it's because she's trying to prove to herself that she can maintain a normal sex life. Sometimes, I don't give a rat's ass what she's trying to prove and hold her because I'm not about to hurt her if I think she's flared up in pain.

"I'm fine," she says, reading my mind. "I just need you."

I prowl onto the bed and half lie on top of her. Our lips meet for a sweet kiss. The moment her tongue seeks out mine, the kiss turns feral and hungry. Her fingernails dig into me as she urges me closer. I settle between her legs, rubbing my cock along her clit. She shudders with pleasure. My thumb and finger tweak her nipple, bringing the good kind of pain to the surface.

"Mmm," she moans.

I give her nipple a hard tug and nip at her bottom lip. "Tell me when you're about to come, angel," I growl. "And then I'm going to slide inside you so

I can feel how good it is to have you gripping my cock. I fucking love when you go crazy for my dick."

She laughs. "I almost think I love your dirty mouth more."

Lifting up, I put space between us so we can stare at the way my thick dick pushes between her pussy lips, rubbing against her nub.

"Look how fucking sexy we are," I tell her. "You and me. Hot as hell."

My words have another moan escaping her. Then, she warns me she's about to come. I grip my cock and slide it between her pussy lips, entering into her tight body. Slowly. It's best when I give her time to adjust to my size. Plus, if she's hurting, the last thing I want to do is start fucking shit up worse.

"Harder," she breathes.

It's her lying voice, though.

In and out, I stroke slowly, letting her get used to me. "Want me to stop?"

"Fuck no," she hisses, her wild eyes pinning me. "Just like this is perfect."

I smirk at her. "Touch your clit, angel. I want to watch."

Her hand slides between us as she works herself close to the edge. She's wet and her juices coat my cock, making it easier to drive into her. When I can tell she's getting tired and weak, I grip her hand in mine and force her body to yield to the orgasm it desperately wants. She screams out my name, her cunt clenching around me, and I lose it. I groan, grinding my release into her until I'm spent and sated. Sliding out of her body, I fall next to her and bury my nose in her hair.

"You okay?"

"Always with you."

"I'm going to do better tomorrow," I vow. "I promise. No more whiskey. You're right. You need me and that shit solves nothing."

"Oh my God," she exclaims.

I sit up, frowning. "What?"

"We need to call someone."

"Who?"

"The press."

I arch a brow. Fucking smartass.

Her lips curl into a mischievous grin. "You said I was right."

"That's all you heard from that entire monologue?"

"Yep. Say it again."

"You're right." I brush a blond strand of hair away from her face. "Your turn."

"But you're never right so…" She laughs.

"Say what I want to hear."

Her brown eyes gleam with wickedness. "You have the best cock in all the land."

"Say the other thing," I murmur, pressing my lips to hers.

"I love you, husband."

"That's the one. I love you too, wife."

CHAPTER
eighteen

Lauren

"Thank you," I tell Enzo, hugging his neck. "It means a lot for you to bring him."

He pats my back. "I'm doing what I can for you guys. Don't worry. These things have a way of working themselves out."

"Score!" Taylor yells.

Daniel shakes his head as he chases after the ping-pong ball. "I'm too old to keep chasing these balls."

Taylor snorts. "He said balls."

I giggle. "He totally did."

Daniel snags the ball up and gives us both one of his perfected "dad stares." It only makes Taylor and me laugh more. While Daniel gets ready to serve, I sit down on the couch in our game room and Enzo plops down beside me. Since he's a social worker, he got a sanctioned visit for us with Taylor. Daniel and I talked about fostering, but it doesn't feel like enough. But before we drag this kid into yet another home, we wanted to see how he feels about it. It doesn't matter what we want if he's not into the idea.

They play until Taylor wins the match and it's nearing time for dinner. Daniel sits in an armchair and Taylor chooses to sit on my other side. I give him a side hug.

"Did you like hanging out with us?" I ask.

He looks up at me, a big grin on his face. "Better than listening to Vera yell at the people reporting the news."

"How would you feel about living here all the time?" Enzo asks, his tone gentle and curious.

Taylor frowns, making my heart plummet. "I don't want to."

Tears well in my eyes, but I force a smile. "It's okay."

"I just…" Taylor looks down at his hands. "I just wouldn't want to leave. I think it will hurt too much."

Daniel slides out of his chair and sits on his knees in front of Taylor. "What if we kept you forever?"

Taylor jerks his head my way. "Forever?" Then he frowns again. "I'm sick, though. People don't want a sick kid."

A tear races down my cheek. "Do you think a healthy kid wants a sick mom?"

He scowls. "Any kid would be lucky to have you as a mom."

"But not you?" I challenge, another tear leaking out.

His bottom lip wobbles. "Especially me, but..." He starts to cry. "I don't want to get my hopes up."

I hug him to me. "We want you to be ours, Taylor. We'll make it happen as long as you want this."

"I do," he sobs. "So much."

When we pull apart, Daniel takes his hand and then takes mine. "Being sick doesn't make you less of a person or any less deserving of a family."

"What happens if I get worse?" Taylor asks, frowning.

"Then you have us to get you through it," Daniel says. And then he winks. "I may be Dr. Dum-Dum, but I know a thing or two about helping sick patients."

"So what do you say?" I urge, smiling at him. "Want to be sick together and make this old man wait on us hand and foot?"

He giggles. "Would I be Taylor Dum-Dum?"

"Totally. You don't think I'd be the only one taking that silly last name, do you?" I tease, tickling him.

"Hey now," Daniel says. "Dum-Dum has a nice ring to it."

"Yes," Taylor agrees. "I want to live with you guys. Even if I have to change my last name to Noodle Butt."

"You said butt." I snort.

Enzo chuckles. "You definitely fit in with these two clowns, Tay."

Taylor simply beams.

And all the broken parts in my body don't matter because my heart just got fuller.

∾

"Do you think they're coming?" I ask, chewing on my bottom lip.

Daniel lifts his brows. "You really think they wouldn't?"

I force out a laugh. Truth is, I don't know. Dad and Landon were so stoic when I told them about my being added to the transplant list. Quiet and almost emotionless. To their defense, I dropped it like a bomb and then had to get to class. It's been a week since I told them and a lot has happened. My life has been a whirlwind of readying our house for Taylor.

He'll be ours soon.

Officially.

We've filed all the paperwork, went through the appropriate channels, and done the home study. It helps knowing a social worker, a few really good attorneys, and a judge. Daniel is well-connected in this community and when he needs a favor, they all come through to make it happen. Once the paperwork is complete, we'll pick up Taylor and bring him here for good.

I'm thrilled.

And nervous.

I don't know anything about being a mom. All I can do is try to be half the mom my own mother was and I feel like I'll do okay. Plus, no one gets Taylor like I do. We connect on a level no one else does. He's my dialysis buddy.

"They better hurry up," I grumble. "Chicken is almost done."

Daniel hugs me to him. "They're coming."

I'm just pulling away when I hear my dad's voice. "Lauren!"

I jolt and turn just in time to see Dad barreling for me. He nearly tackles me with a hug. His grip is tight as he lifts me off the ground.

"Dad!" I cry out. "What's gotten into you?"

"He won," Landon says, entering in behind him.

"Won what?" I ask.

Dad finally releases me and yanks a folded piece of paper out. His eyes are wet with tears as he unfolds it. It's not the same paperwork Daniel received, as his was a simple blood test that showed we were incompatible. This paperwork is a genetic tissue typing blood test result issued from my transplant coordinator.

"I was a fifty percent match," Landon boasts, "but Dad still won."

I blink in confusion.

"The best match for the recipient is six out of six antigens matching," Dad says with a wide, teary smile.

"A zero mismatch," Daniel utters from nearby.

"All six markers match," Dad says, kissing my forehead. "You're getting a kidney, baby girl."

I'm frozen.

Stunned.

Simultaneously upset and overjoyed.

"Daddy…" I choke out a sob.

"Don't say a word, sweetheart," Dad says, pulling me back to his chest. "The transplant coordinator said we're not out of the clear, but we're off to one helluva start."

I cry. I cry and cry and cry. I'm not sure I'll ever stop crying.

My dad is going to give me a kidney.

My dad is my hero.

I'm eventually pulled away so my brother can hug me.

"I was close," he says, his voice husky. "You know I'd give you my left nut if I needed to." Sure, he jokes, but he's crying too.

I look over Landon's shoulder to see Daniel hugging Dad. Not a son-in-law simply hugging his father-in-law. No, he hugs him like he's his hero too.

Hope teases me and I shouldn't take the bait.

Hope is dangerous.

But without hope, what am I even living for?

Hope and I are about to become best friends because I have too many people holding onto hope too. Maybe if we all cling desperately enough, hope will turn into reality.

I need a win.

I *will* win.

Momma didn't raise a quitter.

CHAPTER
nineteen

Daniel

Two months later...

"Go fish, got my wish," Taylor chirps from beside me in the waiting room. "I win again."

I ruffle his blond hair. "You win every time, Noodle Butt."

"It's because I'm better, Dum-Dum Dad."

He always calls me Daniel or Dr. Dum-Dum. This is new. I try to play it off like it's not a big deal, but my heart soars. And I really need my heart to soar because I'm stressed as fuck.

"You're pretty amazing," I agree, swallowing down my emotion.

He's ours on paper. A son. Incredible. But I was prepared for him to call me Daniel for the rest of his life. Not Dad. I didn't want to pressure him. But I sure as hell won't try and stop him.

"Mom's going to be okay," he tells me in a matter-of-fact tone.

My heart burns inside my chest and I fight tears, nodding at him.

"He's right," my mom says as she sits down on my other side. "Our girl's a fighter."

That she is.

I lift my gaze and catch Landon's from across the room. He's pale with dark circles under his eyes. Callie and her dad, August, are sitting beside him in support. The two people Landon loves most are in that operating room. I want to pull him into my arms and thank him for letting his dad go in there with her, but I don't want to embarrass him. Plus, he has his support network and I have a little boy who needs me to be strong.

Time passes too slowly, but thankfully I have Gold Fish on the iPad to entertain me. Taylor whips my ass every round, much to his delight. Just when I'm about to climb the walls with anxiety, Dr. Davis, the surgeon, strides down the hall. I toss the iPad in Mom's lap and jog over to him. Landon is hot on my heels.

"Surgery went well," he assures me, smiling. "Of course only time will tell if it'll be rejected or not, but there's no reason why the transplant won't take. And while we were in there, we performed a nephrec-tomy on the damaged kidney since it was causing so much trouble. As you know, it's common to leave the diseased organs in there, but it was extremely large and overrun by cysts, so in order to make room, it needed to be removed."

By removing the problem kidney, this could mean she'll be pain free one day.

"How is Teddy?"

"He's been in SICU for a while now. Lauren just came out. In another hour or two…" he trails off, smirking. "In another hour or two the family can come in to see them one at a time. But doctors, on the other hand, they have free rein as far as I'm concerned." He winks at me before walking off.

I grip Landon's shoulder. "I'll text you and let you know how they're doing."

As if my ass is on fire, I rush down the hallway to SICU, stopping by my office to grab a lab coat. A nurse lets me into the surgical intensive care unit and I head up to the front desk where a familiar head nurse named Mae is writing something in a chart.

"Dr. Venable," she greets in her no-nonsense tone, not lifting her gaze. "You're not supposed to be in the SICU." She finally looks up and cocks an eyebrow up as she scrutinizes me. This woman runs a tight ship, but she's not immune to my good boy charm. I flash her a winning smile. "Oh, please, honey, like I ever had a chance of denying you access back here. Now Morris, on the other hand." She tsks. "That boy is something else. Curtains two and three, hon."

"Thanks, Mae."

I rush over to curtain two. Lauren is being looked over by a male nurse. She's still out of it as she comes off the anesthetic. I grab her hand and kiss her forehead.

"How is she?" I ask, my voice gruff.

"Vitals are good. Dr. Davis explained that surgery was a success?"

"He did."

"She's a trooper."

Someone loudly moans one curtain over. "Laurennnn." Teddy.

I leave my wife to go check on her father. He's lucid, but his eyes are wild. Rushing over to him, I grip his hand.

"She's okay, Teddy. Lauren is right next door. Surgery was a success for both of you. They took out the diseased kidney too."

He smiles and closes his eyes. Tears leak out of the corners of his eyes. "My baby girl is okay." He scratches at his arm, frowning. "I itch. Why do I itch?" His unfocused eyes meet mine again, confusion swimming in them.

"You might be having a reaction to the morphine," I say, peeking my head out of the curtain. "Mae, can you come here?"

Mae makes her way over to his bed and checks his chart. "Teddy Bear, we're going to switch you to a different pain medication. Okay, honey?"

He doesn't answer, simply claws at his arm some more. As soon as she scurries off, I take his hand again and pull out my phone with the other.

"Where's my baby boy?" Teddy asks, his brows pinched.

"He's waiting outside. He'll come see you soon. I'm texting him now to let him know you're okay. Anything you want me to tell him?"

He nods but doesn't say anything, his eyes drooping. I quickly fire off a text to Landon to let him know his dad loves him. I'm sure if he'd stayed awake long enough, he would've told me. When Mae comes over to give him some meds, I slip away to check on Lauren again.

I sit with her for what feels like a long time, my anxiety high, until I hear it.

A whimper.

A soft cry.

Her beautiful face crumples as she comes to.

"Shhh," I coo. "You made it, angel."

"It hurts," she whispers.

Mae walks over and checks her vitals. I can't take my eyes off my wife's face. She made it through. They both made it through.

"I'm going to get you some more pain meds, hon," Mae promises. "Let this good doctor take care of you."

I pull Lauren's hand up and kiss the back of it before letting it rest. As she comes off the anesthesia, she becomes crabby and teary. Back and forth I go check on her and her father until Teddy gets discharged to a room. They push his bed past hers and stop it where she can see him.

"I love you, Daddy," she chokes out. "Thank you."

He smiles despite the pain he's in. "Anything for you, baby girl."

They steer his bed away.

"Where's my boy?" Her brown eyes are filled with tears. "Where's Taylor?"

I grin at her. "Probably beating his new grandma's ass on Gold Fish."

"He's really good at that game." She closes her eyes and smiles. "Landon?"

"Landon's good. Everyone is here."

"Jenna?"

"Cora's sick, so they're keeping her home. The last thing we need is you or Teddy catching something."

She drifts off and I keep staring at her. So beautiful. Alive. Mine.

I'm in a zone when I hear a familiar voice.

"Awww, come on, Mae-Mae. You love me."

"Boy, I will whoop your ass."

I bite back a snort. Morris.

Leaving Lauren for a moment, I walk over to where Morris is leaned against the nurse station, smirking at Mae. She has her hands on her hips, shaking her head at him.

"Mae's mean," he tattles when I walk up. "How's your girl?"

"She's great. Perfect. And leave Mae alone," I chide.

She nods. "Listen to the good doctor."

"And what am I? The bad doctor?"

"You're the dumbass doctor, boy. Get it right."

"You keep calling me boy and I gotta say, Mae, I'm into it." He waggles his brows at her. "How's Monique? You want to let me take her out?"

"She already has a man, hon."

"Ehh, she's hot, though."

"Monique is a diva, boy. She'd chew you up and swallow you whole."

"Again, Mae, I'm totally into it." He laughs.

"You're into everything, freak," I playfully grumble. "Leave Mae alone and come say hello to Lauren."

I drag him away before Mae decides to knock his ass out. And I wouldn't put it past her either. He sobers up when he sees Lauren, slipping into concerned doctor mode.

"They took the kidney or leave it in?"

"He took it."

"I'm no surgeon, but I would have done the same," he says in agreement. "How you doing, Barbie?"

She cracks her eyes open and manages to flip him off. He and I both laugh to see that her sense of humor is already returning.

A weight that has been crushing me since the day I laid eyes on the beautiful, but sick girl, finally lifts. I pull out a root beer sucker and place it in her hand. Brown eyes meet mine and she smiles.

"Thanks, Dr. Dum-Dum."

$\sim$

"I'm winning," Lauren says, wincing when she looks over her shoulder at her dad.

"Then it's a good thing I'm here instead of Landon," Teddy replies with a chuckle that makes him flinch in pain. "I'd never hear the end of it."

"Awww, poor Dad. Losing to a girl." Her eyes flash with triumph when she slowly makes it to the end of the hall to me.

"Be nice to him," I tell her, collecting her in my arms. "He's an *old* man."

The old man manages to flip me the bird, making me laugh.

It's been two days since the surgery. They're supposed to be walking around as Teddy leaves soon. And while Lauren seemingly is doing better, she requires a little more recovery time.

"Here," I say, handing two suckers to Lauren and kissing her lips. "Give one of these to your dad whenever he makes it here. I need to get back to work."

After a quick wave, I head back down to the ER. Before I round the corner, a little black boy about seven or eight comes around the corner. When he sees me, he grins.

"Hi," he says, waving his hand hard. "I'm Derek. I have a metal leg. I'm part robot."

"Hi, Robot Derek. I'm Dr. Dum-Dum."

He cheeses at me. His eyes are slightly crossed, but he seems to see just fine.

"Are you lost?" I ask, looking around for a parent.

"I'm looking for my dinosaur friend. We brought him here, but it's taking a long time," he explains. "I miss my dinosaur friend."

"Oh yeah? What's your friend's name? I can help you look for him."

"Ollie. He has a dinosaur egg helmet." Then, he tries to whisper, but his voice still carries. "Ollie has epilepsy and hits his head a lot. That's why we're here."

I remember Ollie. The kid from the bookstore.

"There you are," Anna scolds, looking frazzled. "You can't run off like that, Derek. I thought some-one stole you!"

"How about you stay here and I'll go check on Ollie, okay?" I reach into my pocket and pull out a cherry Dum-Dum. "You like suckers?"

He beams. "I love suckers."

"I'll be right back," I promise.

Once in triage, I hunt down Lin to see if she can help me find Ollie. After a quick update by her and I peek at his chart, she points to the fourth room and I head that way. Ollie, not wearing his normal helmet, lies in the bed with tears in his eyes.

"Hey, Mr. Dinosaur," I say, waving as I enter.

His eyes light up. "Dr. Venable!"

"How are you doing, kiddo?" I ask, sitting at the foot of his bed.

"I want to go back to Anna's and color with my best friend Derek. We're making a comic book about a dinosaur and a robot." He smiles at me. "Can you give me a sucker to make me feel better and I can leave?"

I pull out a sucker and hand it to him. Blue raspberry. "Tell you what. I'll see what I can do, okay? We just want to make sure you're feeling okay before we send you away. Even dinosaur boys need checkups."

Morris waltzes in and winks when he sees me. "Nurse Lin said she could part with a juice or a Jell-O, but not both," he says, setting a juice in Ollie's lap. Then, he pulls out a Jell-O from his pocket. "Our secret, little man. I got you both. She doesn't know you're part dinosaur."

Ollie is happy, so I leave him with Morris and make my way back out to Anna, who's now in the waiting room with Derek and three other kids. Her patience seems to be wearing thin and two kids are pouting beside her, seemingly in time-out.

"Ollie is doing great. Eating Jell-O and making friends," I tell Derek. Then, to Anna I say, "Can we talk a sec?"

She nods. "If I catch you two fighting again, I'll be calling your caseworker. You know I don't tolerate fighting." The two boys around twelve scowl at her.

I walk her away from the kids and give her the

rundown on his results. She is only halfway listening and when the boys start fighting again, she is on the move, whipping out her phone to call the caseworker.

I let out a heavy sigh. "Does anyone care about him?" I mutter to myself.

"I do," Derek says. "When he gets better, we're going to run away."

Squatting down in front of him, I frown. "Why's that, Robot Derek?"

"Because the other kids are mean," Derek explains. "I know you think because I have cerebral palsy that I can't run." He lifts his chin. "I can run really fast."

"Anna seems nice," I tell him. "Have you talked to her?"

"Anna doesn't love us," Derek replies, his eyes crossing harder when tears form. "We're going to go on a hunt."

"A hunt?"

"For people who do."

I scrub my palm down my face, trying to chase away the ache inside me. For so long I went through life focused on my career and not much else. Then Jenna came into my life. A daughter. My heart cracked open then, and I started to not just live, but love. And now that my heart is open and ready, that love isn't isolated to a daughter or a wife. It's spreading like a fire, flaming wider and reaching for those who need the warmth.

Like Taylor Dum-Dum.

It makes me wonder if Robot Derek and Mr. Dinosaur want to be Dum-Dums with us too.

"Can I tell you a secret?" I smile at Derek.

"I like secrets."

"This secret is really important. Only you and Ollie can know it."

He nods, smiling, no longer teary-eyed.

"There're people out there who will love you," I assure him. "And you won't have to look for them. They'll come to you."

"How do you know this?"

"Because it happened to me. That's how I found my daughter and my wife. And my son Taylor."

"Wow, cool," he breathes.

"And if you run away, they may not be able to find you." I stand and pat his head. "Can you promise me something, Robot Derek?"

"Yes."

"Promise me you won't run away. Promise me you'll let them find you."

His face falls, but he nods. "I hope they don't take too long. We're lonely."

"You have each other," I assure him. "But don't worry, they're out there looking for you right now."

epilogue

Lauren

One year later…

Someone giggles and I lift a brow, fighting a smile. "I heard that," I say with mock gruffness. "You're supposed to be studying. All of you."

They all burst out laughing at once and I can't ignore it this time. I start laughing too. At this rate, we'll never get our homework done.

"You guys are a bad influence," I tell them.

"Maybe we should eat ice cream instead of working," Taylor offers. "Dad bought root beer. We could have root beer floats."

"Yeah!" Ollie and Derek say in unison.

Root beer.

It's my weakness.

And, thankfully, one of my few weaknesses these days thanks to my transplant.

"Fine," I huff. "We'll have root beer floats, but whoever tells Dad has to do dishes for a week."

"Tell Dad what?" Daniel asks, sauntering into the kitchen wearing a smirk.

"I give up," I groan.

All three boys giggle again. It's the sweetest sound in the world.

"Root beer floats instead of homework, I gather?" Daniel asks as he starts pulling out the ice cream and soda.

The boys abandon me at the kitchen table to help. They circle around Daniel, eager and excited. I can't help but watch them.

Our boys.

When I was home recovering, Daniel brought something up to me. Two foster boys who were best buds. Two little guys who needed love—a love only we could give. My new kidney may have been working like a champ, but my heart broke for them. As soon as I met Robot Derek and saw Mr. Dinosaur again, I had an overwhelming urge to love and protect them. Jenna calls it a motherly instinct, and apparently I have one. We did what we had to do amidst my healing and made it happen.

They're ours now.

Just like Taylor.

My three little bears.

And their momma feels incredible. She's never going to leave them, no matter what her future health throws at her. Never.

Daniel is handsome today, having just come home from work. He still wears a tie and a nice shirt, but he's since rolled up his sleeves to keep from getting ice cream on them. His smile is crooked and silly as he chats with the boys about their day. I could stare at my family forever. They're perfect. More than I could have ever dreamed up for myself.

I've given up on homework and close my psychology textbook. I should be worrying about what I'll cook for supper tonight, but I can't find it in me to worry. Not when I can watch my boys as they babble about how they each think root beer floats came into existence.

"It was aliens," Derek says, deadly serious. "I saw it on YouTube."

Daniel shakes his head. "You can't believe everything on the Internet."

"Oh boy," Taylor groans. "Here we go again."

They continue to argue, but Ollie slips away to bring me a root beer float. It's messy and dripping all over my newly mopped floors, but I don't mind. It's the thought that counts. His helmet is in place and I'm happy he's wearing it. Though he's had less seizures the older he gets, he still hasn't been cleared to not wear it as often. I hug him to me and he nuzzles his face into my hair.

"I love you, Momma," he says, melting my heart. "Thank you for finding us."

My eyes burn with tears as I pat his back. "I love you too, baby."

We're still hugging when I feel eyes on me. My

stare meets Daniel's. He's watching me with an intensity that always turns my insides to mush.

You're a good mother.

He says it all the time, but more importantly, he makes me feel it.

"Okay, Mr. Dinosaur," I chirp, to chase away the urge to cry with happiness. "Let's have a taste of this amazing root beer float."

Ollie and I take turns sipping on the yummy treat.

"Best root beer float ever," I praise.

"Mom," Taylor says, "try mine."

I have a taste of his. "Ohhhh, we have a competition now."

Ollie giggles. "What does the winner get?"

"Kisses," I tell them primly. "Lots of kisses."

"Momma, taste this one," Derek says, hobbling over to us, sloshing the root beer all over the floor.

"Careful not to slip," I say as I take the cup from him. After a sip, I nod. "Oooh, this is great!"

I'm pretending to decide which one I like best when Daniel comes around my other side and kneels. He hands me a root beer float with a root beer Dum-Dum unwrapped with the stick down inside the straw.

The boys all laugh and call him a cheater.

I pull out the Dum-Dum and have a taste. Then I sip down the root beer. "Ding-ding-ding! We have a winner."

Daniel leans in for his kiss and I give him a long one.

One that says I love you.

One that says thank you.

One that makes the boys groan and call us gross.

When he pulls away, I can't help but bask in the moment. That's all life is anyway. A series of moments all smashed together to make one incredible journey. Sometimes the journey is short, and other times it's long. It doesn't matter the duration, but how much fun you have along the way. It should be filled with love, laughter, and end with root beer floats.

But our story doesn't end here.

Dr. Dum-Dum and Root Beer Angel have more love to give to other little souls like Noodle Butt and Robot Derek and Mr. Dinosaur.

We just have to find them first.

Daniel

"Well, if it isn't the good doctor," Mae says when I charge into the SICU.

"Just checking on my patient." My voice is tight. I'm stressed as fuck. We almost lost her. Lin cried when they wheeled her off the OR.

"Princess Nakayla is sleeping it off, hon. Want me to call you when she's being moved to PICU?"

She knows better. I won't rest until I see that she's okay. The tiny thing had emergency heart surgery, for fuck's sake. I need to see her.

Mae lets out a heavy sigh. "You remind me of my granddaughter. She has a heart of gold and a spine of steel. Relentless as hell. That's why you're my favorite and you get away with so much when it comes to me. Go on, she's in curtain six."

I give her a thankful smile before stalking over to where the little girl sleeps. Her chocolate-brown skin is a contrast against the white sheets. My own heart cracks right down the middle seeing her sleeping so serenely on the bed with tubes and wires coming out of her.

"Hey, little princess," I whisper as I sit on the edge of the bed. "How are you doing?"

I doubt she can hear me, but I don't want her to be alone. Not now. Not after nearly dying today. Her brown cheeks are still streaked from her crying when they first brought her in. At just two, she's so fragile and tiny. I wish I could call her mother in here and force her to cuddle her.

But she has no mother.

I tore apart her file the moment she was whisked off to the OR. Nakayla Dawson lives with Anna. Another foster kid. Broken and abandoned. Lost.

"She looks like a princess, hmm?" Mae asks as she flits around and checks her vitals.

"She does," I say, my voice husky with emotion. "What did Dr. Davis say?"

"He repaired the atrial septal defect without open-heart surgery. Was able to patch it," she says, stopping to stroke her fingers over the toddler's forehead. "She should make a full recovery, but as with any condition, she'll need to have it continually monitored."

I'm still staring at Nakayla long after Mae leaves. The little girl's eyes eventually flutter open. Big, round, pale brown. As soon as she sees me, her eyes fill with tears. Her bottom lip wobbles.

"Aww, don't cry, little princess," I say softly, patting her foot over the blanket. "I'm a doctor. You're safe here."

"B-Bankie," she whispers, her voice so sad and sweet.

"You want your blankie?"

She nods, sending tears cascading down her brown cheeks. Nakayla is the cutest little girl.

"Tell you what," I say as a nurse comes in. "I'm going to go look for your blankie."

Nakayla starts to cry, effectively breaking my heart. "Dotor no bye-bye."

I shoot the nurse a panicked look and he laughs. "I'll go out there and look for it."

"I'm not going anywhere," I assure her. "The nurse is going to get it."

She smiles shyly. Such a beautiful smile.

Reminds me of my granddaughter Cora when I'd first met her.

"Do you like suckers?"

She nods, watching me curiously.

I reach into my pocket and pull out a bubble-gum-flavored Dum-Dums sucker. Her brown eyes widen.

"Peek," she squeaks out. "Peek sucker."

"You like pink?"

"Pink bankie."

"My wife likes pink," I tell her as I hand her the sucker. "She's the only girl in a house full of boys."

Nakayla kicks at the blanket and sticks her small foot out to show me. She wiggles her toes, showing me they're painted pink. She clutches the sucker but doesn't try to eat it.

"Those are the prettiest toes I've ever seen."

The nurse returns with a ratty pink blanket that's seen better days. Nakayla snatches it and hugs it to her. In one hand, she clutches the bubblegum sucker and then she shoves her thumb into her mouth. Her lids droop and then she startles awake.

"Dotor no bye-bye," she says firmly, around her thumb she's sucking.

I pat her cute brown foot before covering it back up with the blanket. "Dr. Dum-Dum's not going anywhere."

She smiles and then starts to fall asleep. As soon as her eyes are closed, I pull out my phone and text Lauren.

Me: We need a princess.

My wife immediately responds.

Lauren: Did you find a missing part of our family?

Me: When you know, you know.

Lauren: What's her name?

Me: Nakayla. She loves pink.

Lauren: I think Nakayla Venable has a lovely ring to it. I'll call Enzo and get the ball rolling. Love you, Dr. Dan.

Me: Love you too, angel.

Nakayla sucks on her thumb, looking sweet and serene. She may have a literally broken heart, but the Venable family is just the one to fix it. Alone, we're sad and broken, but together we're strong and happy. She deserves to be loved and happy too.

Sometimes the best medicine isn't anything that can be prescribed.

But love can be a healer.

I should know. I'm a doctor.

The End

If you enjoyed Daniel and Lauren in *Dr. Dan*, you'll love Drew and Sophia in *Crybaby*!

K WEBSTER'S Taboo World

Cast of Characters

Brandt Smith (Rick's Best Friend)
Kelsey McMahon (Rick's Daughter)
Rick McMahon (Sheriff)
Mandy Halston (Kelsey's Best Friend)

Miles Reynolds (Drew's Best Friend)
Olivia Rowe (Max's Daughter/Sophia's Sister)

Dane Alexander (Max's Best Friend)
Nick Stratton

Judge Maximillian "Max" Rowe (Olivia and Sophia's
Father)
Dorian Dresser

Drew Hamilton (Miles's Best Friend)
Sophia Rowe (Max's Daughter/Olivia's Sister)

Easton McAvoy (Preacher)
Lacy Greenwood (Stephanie's Daughter)

Stephanie Greenwood (Lacy's Mother)
Anthony Blakely (Quinn's Son)
Aiden Blakely (Quinn's Son)

Quinn Blakely (Anthony and Aiden's Father)
Ava Prince (Lacy/Raven/Olivia's Friend)

Karelma Bonilla (Mateo's Daughter)
Adam Renner (Principal)

Coach Everett Long (Adam's Friend)
River Banks (Olivia's Best Friend)

Mateo Bonilla (Four Fathers Series Side Character)

Vaughn Young
Vale Young

Enzo Tauber
Jenna Pruitt (Dr. Venable's Daughter)

August Miller
Winter Burke

Callie Miller (August's Daughter)
Landon Englewood (Lauren's Brother)

Teddy Englewood (Landon and Lauren's Dad)

Lauren Englewood
Daniel Venable (ER Doctor and Jenna's Father)

acknowledgements

Thank you to my wonderful husband, Matt, who encourages me to "write better books" and keeps me humble. Also, he listens to each and every storyline without fail, always offering unique advice that I never take…HA!

A huge thank you to my Krazy for K Webster's Books readers group. You all are insanely supportive and I can't thank you enough.

Thanks so much to Misty Walker for being the best friend a girl could ask for!

Lauren, the real Lauren, thank you for answering all of my questions about kidney disease and generously offering me your own story. I hope I did this Lauren justice and honored you in a way that makes your heart happy! #LaurenIsAFighter

A gigantic thank you to those who always help me out. Elizabeth Clinton, Ella Stewart, Misty Walker, Holly Sparks, Jillian Ruize, Gina Behrends, and Wendy Rinebold—you ladies are amazing!

A big thank you to my author friends who have given me your friendship and your support. You have no idea how much that means to me.

Thank you to all my blogger friends both big and small that go above and beyond to always share my stuff. You all rock! #AllBlogsMatter

Emily with Lawrence Editing, thank you SO much for editing this book. You rock!!

Thank you Stacey Blake for your artistic magic, always pleasant attitude, and ongoing professionalism. I appreciate you more than you could ever know! My books are always formatted so beautifully thanks to you! Love you, lady!

A big thanks to Nicole Blanchard with IndieSage PR for always taking care of me. You're a doll and I love you!

Lastly but certainly not least of all, thank you to all of the wonderful readers out there who are willing to hear my stories and enjoy the characters like I do. It means the world to me!

about the author

K Webster is a *USA Today* Bestselling author. Her titles have claimed many bestseller tags in numerous categories, are translated in multiple languages, and have been adapted into audiobooks. She lives in "Tornado Alley" with her husband, two children, and her baby dog named Blue. When she's not writing, she's reading, drinking copious amounts of coffee, and researching aliens.

Keep up with K Webster

Facebook:
www.facebook.com/authorkwebster

Blog:
authorkwebster.wordpress.com

Twitter:
twitter.com/KristiWebster

Email:
kristi@authorkwebster.com

Goodreads:
www.goodreads.com/user/show/10439773-k-webster

Instagram:
instagram.com/kristiwebster

BookBub:
www.bookbub.com/authors/k-webster

books by
K WEBSTER

Psychological Romance Standalones:
My Torin
Whispers and the Roars
Cold Cole Heart
Blue Hill Blood

Romantic Suspense Standalones:
Dirty Ugly Toy
El Malo
Notice
Sweet Jayne
The Road Back to Us
Surviving Harley
Love and Law
Moth to a Flame
Erased

Extremely Forbidden Romance Standalones:
The Wild
Hale
Like Dragonflies

Contemporary Romance Standalones:
Wicked Lies Boys Tell
The Day She Cried
Untimely You
Heath
Sundays are for Hangovers
A Merry Christmas with Judy
Zeke's Eden
Schooled by a Senior
Give Me Yesterday
Sunshine and the Stalker
Bidding for Keeps
B-Sides and Rarities

Paranormal Romance Standalones:
Apartment 2B
Running Free
Mad Sea

War & Peace Series:
This is War, Baby (Book 1)
This is Love, Baby (Book 2)
This Isn't Over, Baby (Book 3)
This Isn't You, Baby (Book 4)
This is Me, Baby (Book 5)
This Isn't Fair, Baby (Book 6)
This is the End, Baby (Book 7 – a novella)

Lost Planet Series:
The Forgotten Commander (Book 1)
The Vanished Specialist (Book 2)
The Mad Lieutenant (Book 3)
The Uncertain Scientist (Book 4)

2 Lovers Series:
Text 2 Lovers (Book 1)
Hate 2 Lovers (Book 2)
Thieves 2 Lovers (Book 3)

Pretty Little Dolls Series:
Pretty Stolen Dolls (Book 1)
Pretty Lost Dolls (Book 2)
Pretty New Doll (Book 3)
Pretty Broken Dolls (Book 4)

The V Games Series:
Vlad (Book 1)
Ven (Book 2)
Vas (Book 3)

Four Fathers Books:
Pearson

Four Sons Books:
Camden

Elite Seven Books:
Gluttony
Greed

Not Safe for Amazon Books:
The Wild
Hale
Bad Bad Bad
This is War, Baby
Like Dragonflies

The Breaking the Rules Series:
Broken (Book 1)
Wrong (Book 2)
Scarred (Book 3)
Mistake (Book 4)
Crushed (Book 5 – a novella)

The Vegas Aces Series:
Rock Country (Book 1)
Rock Heart (Book 2)
Rock Bottom (Book 3)

The Becoming Her Series:
Becoming Lady Thomas (Book 1)
Becoming Countess Dumont (Book 2)
Becoming Mrs. Benedict (Book 3)

Alpha & Omega Duet:
Alpha & Omega (Book 1)
Omega & Love (Book 2)

K WEBSTER'S
Taboo World

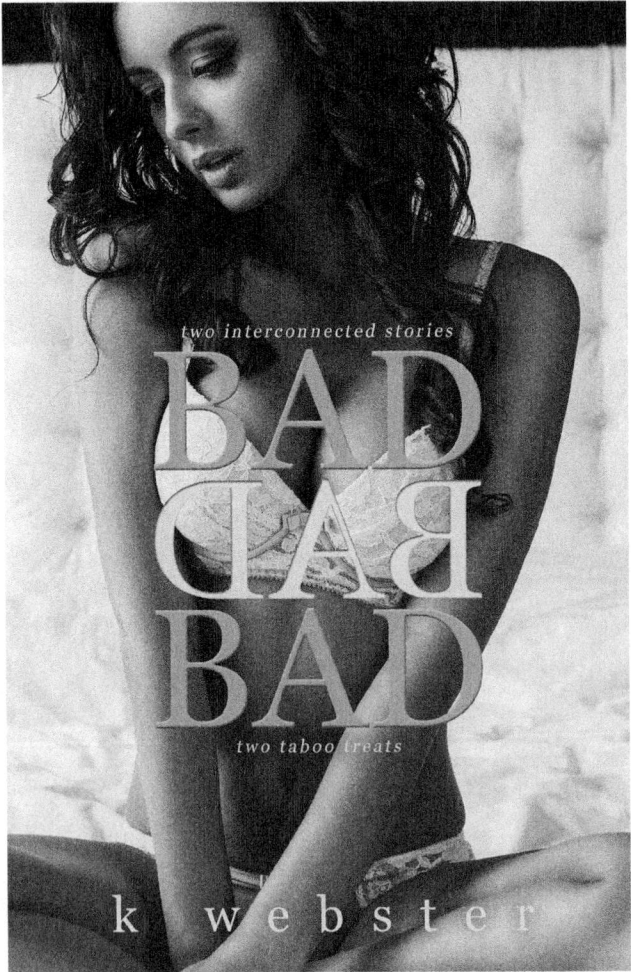

two interconnected stories

BAD
BAD
BAD

two taboo treats

k webster

Bad Bad Bad

Two interconnected stories. Two taboo treats.

Brandt's Cherry Girl

He's old enough to be her father.
She's his best friend's daughter.
Their connection is off the charts.
And so very, very wrong.
This can't happen.
Oh, but it already is…

Sheriff's Bad Girl

He's the law and follows the rules.
She's wild and out of control.
His daughter's best friend is trouble.
And he wants to punish her…
With his teeth.

USA TODAY BESTSELLING AUTHOR
K WEBSTER

She's a hurdle in his way...
and he wants to jump her.

a taboo treat

COACH
LONG

Coach Long

Coach Everett Long has a chip on his shoulder.
Working every day with the man who stole his
fiancée leaves him pissed and on edge.
His temper is volatile and his attitude sucks.

River Banks is a funky-styled runner
with a bizarre past.
Starting over at a new school was supposed to
be easy…but she should have known better.
She likes to antagonize and tends to go after
what she's not supposed to have.

When the arrogant bully meets the strong-willed
brat, it sparks an illicit attraction.
Together, they heat up the track with
longing and desire.
Everything about their chemistry is wrong.
So why does it feel so right?

She's a hurdle in his way and, dear God does
he want to jump her.
Will she be worth the risk or
will he fall flat on his face?

Ex-Rated Attraction

I liked Caleb.

I like his dad more.

Miles Reynolds sent shocks through me the very first time I met him. With his full beard and sculpted ass, he's every inch a heroic, powerful Greek god.

He saved me from a bad situation and now he's all I can think of. Every minute of every hour of every day, I want that man.

He's warned me away, says I can't handle what he has to give.

But I know better.

Miles is exactly what I need—now, then and forever.

Mr. Blakely

It started as a job.

It turned into so much more.

Mr. Blakely is strict with his sons, but he's soft and gentle with me.

The powerful businessman is something else entirely when we're together.

Boss, teacher, lover…husband.

My hopes and dreams for the future have changed. I want—no, I need—him by my side.

a taboo treat

malfeasance

Judge Rowe
never had
a problem with
morality...
until her.

USA TODAY BESTSELLING AUTHOR
K WEBSTER

Malfeasance

Max Rowe always follows the rules.
A successful judge.
A single father.
A leader in the community.
Doing the right thing means everything.

But when he finds himself rescuing an incredibly
young woman,
everything he's worked hard for is quickly forgotten.
The only thing that matters is keeping her safe.
She's gorgeous, intelligent, and the ultimate
temptation.
Doing the wrong thing suddenly feels right.

Their chemistry is intense.
It's a romance no one will approve of, yet one they
can't ignore.
Hot, fast, and explosive.
Someone is going to get burned.

He'll give up everything for her...
because without her, he is nothing.

EASTON

K WEBSTER

Easton

A man who made countless mistakes.
A woman with a messy past.

He's tasked with helping her find her way.
She's lost in grief and self-doubt.

Together they begin something innocent…
Until it's not.

His freedom is at risk.
Her heart won't survive another break.

All rational thinking says they
should stay away from each other.
But neither are very good
at following the rules.

A deep, dark craving.
An overwhelming need.
A burn much hotter than any hell
they could ever be condemned to.

He'll give up everything for her…
because without her, he is nothing.

He likes her screams.
He likes them an awful lot.

Crybaby

a taboo treat

K WEBSTER

Crybaby

Stubborn.
Mouthy.
Brazen.
Two people with vicious tongues.
A desperate temptation neither can ignore.

An injury has changed her entire life.
She's crippled, hopeless, and angry.
And the only one who can lessen her pain is him.

Being the boss is sometimes a pain in the ass.
He's irritated, impatient, and doesn't play games.
Yet he's the only one willing to fight her…for her.

Daring.
Forbidden.
Out of control.
Someone is going to get hurt.
And, oh, how painfully sweet that will be.

The grass is greener where
he points his hose...

lawn
BOYS

a taboo treat

USA TODAY BESTSELLING AUTHOR
K WEBSTER

Lawn Boys

She's lived her life and it has been a good one.
Marriage. College. A family.
Slowly, though, life moved forward and left her at a
standstill.

Until the lawn boy barges into her world.
Bossy. Big. Sexy as hell.
A virile young male to remind her she's all woman.

Too bad she's twice his age.
Too bad he doesn't care.

She's older and wiser and more mature.
Which means absolutely nothing when he's invading
her space.

USA TODAY BESTSELLING AUTHOR

K WEBSTER

Principal Renner,
I've been *bad*.
Again.

a taboo treat

RENNER'S
Rules

Renner's Rules

I'm a bad girl.
I was sent away.
New house. New rules. New school.
Change was supposed to be…good.

Until I met him.

No one warned me Principal Renner would be so
hot.
I'd expected some old, graying man in a brown suit.
Not this.
Not well over six feet of lean muscle and piercing
green eyes.
Not a rugged-faced, ax-wielding lumberjack of a
man.

He's grouchy and rude and likes to boss me around.
I find myself getting in trouble just so he'll punish
me.
Especially with his favorite metal ruler.

Being bad never felt so good

K WEBSTER

Two people.
Their unraveling
marriage.
And they want
me to be...

The

GLUE

a taboo treat

The Glue

I'm a fixer. A lover. Always searching for the right fit.
And I come up empty every time.
My desires are unusual.
I don't feel whole until I'm in the middle, holding it
all together.
Which makes having a romantic relationship really
difficult.

Until them.
Two people. An unraveling marriage. Love on the
rocks.
And they want me.
To put them back together again.

Problem is, once they're fixed, where does that leave
me?
I sure as hell hope I stick like glue.

USA TODAY BESTSELLING AUTHOR

K WEBSTER

He was the boss in
the bedroom.
I was the boss outside of it.
Two alphas.
One hot agenda.

DANE

a taboo treat

Dane

I'm used to being in charge.
In the courtroom. In life. In the bedroom.
But then I met him.

He brings me *literally* to my knees.

Handsome. Charismatic. Sexy as hell.
He's everything I desperately crave to possess.

I'm burning to get him beneath me just to have a
taste.
Turns out, though, one taste isn't enough.
And he's starved for me too.

Two alphas fighting for dominance.
He thrives on control and I can't give it up.

A battle of wills.
The bedroom is the battlefield and our hearts are on
the line.

USA *TODAY* BESTSELLING AUTHOR
K WEBSTER

SHE DOESN'T NEED
A HERO.
SHE JUST NEEDS
HIM.

en
zo

A TABOO TREAT

Enzo

Jenna's grown up in the system.
Forced to be tough, wary, and hard.

She's only been able to count on herself.
Until Enzo.
He's much older and responsible for looking after
her.
What should be a job to him, evolves into much
more.

Late night phone calls.
Lingering touches.
A forbidden fire that burns brighter each day.

Everything about him exudes strength.
His will to protect her is more than she could ever
ask for.
Sadly, though, even heroes have their limitations.

But she doesn't need a hero.
She just needs him.

USA TODAY BESTSELLING AUTHOR
K WEBSTER

He was supposed
to hurt her,
but this
REDHEAD
bites back...

RED
HOT
A TABOO TREAT
WINTER

Red Hot Winter

August is bitter and cold.
Two people he loved most betrayed him.

Winter is hot and sultry.
She's the enemy's daughter.

A blowout fight between Winter and her dad
sends her straight into August's waiting arms.
But August doesn't want to hold her…he wants
revenge.

The two are an explosive combination
whenever they're together. August antagonizes
and Winter pushes back. Under all the hate
burning between them is an attraction so
intense, neither can ignore it.

It's only a matter of time before it consumes
them both.

Printed in Great Britain
by Amazon